Barrington Corporation

Vol.1 No. 5
May 1999

• We can't believe gorgeous hunk
Sam Wainwright is settling down—and
marrying his faithful assistant, Patricia Peel.
Although sources tell us that the hasty union
started as a matter of convenience, close
friends say that the marriage may actually
be based on matters of the heart....

• Is anyone but me wondering what Mike
the mailman was discussing with CEO
Rex Barrington II at Rex's retirement party?
They seemed awfully chummy. Do you
suppose Mike knows some juicy secret
about Rex's mysterious son, "The Third,"
and is holding it over Rex II's head?

• Speaking of "The Third"... Don't
tell anyone but Sophia Shepherd has
been secretly doodling the words
Mrs. Rex Michael Barrington III all over
her notepad. It seems she is determined to
marry "The Third"—just like all of her
friends are marrying their bosses. Could she
be the next bride in the office?

Dear Reader,

As spring turns to summer, make Silhouette Romance the perfect companion for those lazy days and sultry nights! Fans of our LOVING THE BOSS series won't want to miss *The Marriage Merger* by exciting author Vivian Leiber. A pretend engagement between friends goes awry when their white lies lead to a *real* white wedding!

Take one biological-clock-ticking twin posing as a new mom and one daddy determined to gain custody of his newborn son, and you've got the unsuspecting partners in *The Baby Arrangement,* Moyra Tarling's tender BUNDLES OF JOY title. You've asked for more TWINS ON THE DOORSTEP, Stella Bagwell's charming author-led miniseries, so this month we give you *Millionaire on Her Doorstep,* an emotional story of two wounded souls who find love in the most unexpected way...and in the most unexpected place.

Can a bachelor bent on never marrying and a single mom with a bustling brood of four become a *Fairy-Tale Family?* Find out in Pat Montana's delightful new novel. Next, a handsome doctor's case of mistaken identity leads to *The Triplet's Wedding Wish* in this heartwarming tale by DeAnna Talcott. And a young widow finds the home—and family—she's always wanted when she strikes a deal with a *Nevada Cowboy Dad,* this month's FAMILY MATTERS offering from Dorsey Kelley.

Enjoy this month's fantastic selections, and make sure to return each and every month to Silhouette Romance!

Mary-Theresa Hussey

Mary-Theresa Hussey
Senior Editor, Silhouette Romance

Please address questions and book requests to:
Silhouette Reader Service
U.S.: 3010 Walden Ave., P.O. Box 1325, Buffalo, NY 14269
Canadian: P.O. Box 609, Fort Erie, Ont. L2A 5X3

THE MARRIAGE MERGER

Vivian Leiber

Silhouette
R O M A N C E™
Published by Silhouette Books
America's Publisher of Contemporary Romance

Special thanks and acknowledgment
are given to ArLynn Leiber Presser,
writing as Vivian Leiber,
for her contribution to the Loving the Boss miniseries.

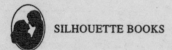 SILHOUETTE BOOKS

ISBN 0-373-19366-1

THE MARRIAGE MERGER

Copyright © 1999 by Harlequin Books S.A.

Look us up on-line at: http://www.romance.net

Printed in U.S.A.

Books by Vivian Leiber

Silhouette Romance

VIVIAN LEIBER

believes that life is full of surprises. When she was old enough to know better about first dates, she met her husband. When she was told by everyone in her family that she was "carrying" like she was having a girl she ended up with Joseph and Eastman. When her boys took an etiquette class, they still ended up putting their elbows on the table (maybe that's not so much of a surprise!). And when she mailed her first manuscript, *Casey's Flyboy,* to Silhouette editor Mary-Theresa Hussey, she was stunned when she got the magic phone call saying "We loved your book!" Since then, her readers have found that while there will always be a happy ending, the way Vivian's characters find their happiness is a tender, heartwarming and delightful surprise.

Marriage Contract

I, Patricia Peel, do hereby agree to temporarily marry my charming and sexy boss, Sam Wainwright. I promise to pose as a loving bride to help him satisfy the company president who is determined to see Sam happily wed. Our marriage shall be strictly in name only—unless, of course, we fall in love.

Patricia Peel

Chapter One

Other women did it. Other women even bragged about it. A poll published in the *Arizona Republic* just the week before showed that a whopping sixty percent of women had done it at least once, sometimes twice. There were even national magazine articles advising women on how to do it. In this modern age, according to the one article Patricia had read after coming home from Olivia McGovern-Hunter's baby shower, a woman who couldn't do it was either hopelessly old-fashioned, dealing with self-esteem issues or was a full-fledged wimp.

"Wimp," Patricia agreed.

Other women asked men out. Other women even proposed marriage. Other women…well, other women did a lot of things Patricia Peel didn't do.

But she was going to do it this morning. She tucked a curl of strawberry blond hair behind her ear, cleared her throat and clasped her hands on her lap so that she wouldn't give in to the urge to bite her nails.

"Sam, I don't approve of affairs," she said, her chin tilted up for emphasis and then dropped in defeat. "Start over. Affairs sounds tawdry. Pick a new word. Sam, neither of us approves of romantic relationships between people who work together. Especially when the man is in a powerful position vis-à-vis the woman. We went to a seminar about that in Washington, remember? Put on by that government lady. The one with the big hair."

Don't get off on a tangent, she warned herself—she and Sam both had joked for days afterward about the size of that woman's hairdo, and mentioning the seminar would only provoke another round of jokes.

Start over.

Patricia pulled all her hair out of her scrunchie and tried to get it all under control in a neat ponytail at her nape. She straightened the file folders on her desk so that the corners were as precisely stacked as the five stories of Barrington Corporation headquarters rising out of the Sonoran Desert on the outskirts of Phoenix. She squared her shoulders, straining the seams of her conservative gray suit that was too hot for the office, even with the generous blast of air-conditioning coming from the floor vents and even with it being early morning when the sun hadn't yet burned the dew.

"Sam, I love you and I have since I took this job

six months ago,'' she said, thinking the simple, straightforward approach might be best. ''You're the reason I took this job—when you interviewed me, I couldn't stop thinking about you. And I had that offer in St. Louis but I didn't take it just because, well, just because of you. I've kept my feelings to myself because you are—I mean, were—engaged. Or at least that's what I've heard. The 'were' part, not the 'are' part.''

She put her hand to her forehead. Why couldn't she get this right?

''What I mean is, that we all know that you're engaged. Were. And don't get me wrong. Melissa's a wonderful woman.''

Patricia bit her lip at this outright lie. The few times Melissa had come to Barrington Corporation to pick up Sam, she had acted in a manner that could best be described as beginning with *b* and rhyming with witch. As Patricia thought about this, she hated her own uncharitable thoughts—wondering, too, how much of her judgment of Melissa was colored by her own...be honest, Patricia warned herself...jealousy.

Plain old-fashioned vegetable-garden-green jealousy.

But the company gossip that was traded at Olivia's baby shower was unequivocal—Melissa and Sam had broken up. While Sam was the vice president of personnel at Barrington Corporation and officially Patricia's boss, he was also an unattached single man—a situation that, given his attractiveness to women, would last a good minute and a half. In fact, Patricia wouldn't have been surprised if she had arrived at work this morning to find a line of beautiful women snaking down the hall from Sam's office. If she had a chance with him, she'd have to act. Now or possibly never.

"I'm really sorry that you and Melissa broke up," Patricia continued raggedly. "Ooooh, that was another lie, wasn't it? And a doozy, too."

She glanced at her watch—9:02.

She picked up the stack of folders on her desk. Fifteen résumés from college students graduating from the best schools. It had been her idea to recruit on the South Florida beach during Spring Break. Sam had been thrilled—it was a great way to meet the applicants in a relaxed, friendly atmosphere. They had made their reservations to coincide with the spring breaks of the major state universities.

Patricia and Sam had been inseparable. Spending their days on the beach, talking with students and handing out brochures about Barrington Corporation's generous benefits packages. Spending their nights at the best restaurants in Fort Lauderdale, reviewing the candidates' résumés. And in between work, there had been play—a snorkeling trip one afternoon, a floor show at the hotel's nightclub, and shooting hoops at the local park's basketball court. She would forget—for hours at a time—that he was engaged, that he was taken, that he thought of her as a pal and a colleague. Not as a woman.

She had come home with fifteen solid job candidates, four snow globes, a lobster-red burn from the one day she forgot to apply sunscreen, and a terrible sense that the best week of her life had just come to a close. Though her skin was back to its pale bisque shade, nothing in the past three months had changed that conviction.

She stood up and walked to the closed door of her office.

"Sam, remember when we went to the Little Havana Nightclub and drank sloe gin fizzes and the showgirls were dressed in rhinestones and feathers? Well, I want to do that again, but not so corporate."

Patricia shook her head. This wasn't going to work. She wasn't the kind of confident, assertive take-no-prisoners woman who could ask a man out. Maybe she was a wimp. There were things that some people might call difficult that she had done without as much anxiety—meeting the French prime minister when she was twelve, curtsying to the queen of Belgium when she was fourteen and making small talk with the president-for-life of Liberia when her parents were posted in Africa.

It's just asking a man to go out on a date.

That was a tough one.

And then there was the down-and-dirty approach.

"I have tickets to the basketball game," she said, her words tumbling out of her mouth with the rapidity of a white-water river. "Two of them. Would you like to join me?"

That wouldn't work. They always went to basketball games together. He wouldn't get the wrong—make that the *right*—idea. In fact, nobody who saw them together in the past year and a half—at parties, at ball games, at museums—ever got the wrong idea.

And that was the problem.

Patricia smoothed her knee-length skirt and strode out of the office—9:03.

She was late and he'd wonder about that—not that he'd disapprove. He'd just want to know—because she was always the dependably punctual one.

"Sam, I just wanted to tell you that I like you."

Well, of course. They were friends as well as co-workers. He wouldn't get it.

"I like you...but not in a friendly way."

That didn't sound good, either.

She stood in the hallway—the soothing turquoise blue walls not doing its soothing job—and held her hand up to knock gently on his door before entering. She squeezed her eyes tight.

"If you don't feel the same way about me, that's okay. It won't affect our working relationship. But I thought I should tell you because...well, because life is so short and I'm already twenty-nine years old, and if you love someone you should let them know. So I'm letting you know, Sam, that I..."

She heard the door hinges squeak. Gulping, Patricia opened her eyes to face an older, yet still trim, man in a pale blue suit. Her heart sunk. His green eyes twinkled mischievously.

"Mr. Barrington, I'm so sorry," Patricia sputtered, keeping her eyes on his red-and-blue tie so that she wouldn't have to look head-on at the president of Barrington Corporation.

"I've always thought that if you love someone you should let them know," Mr. Barrington said, and with a nod goodbye he strode down the hall with all the stately grace of a cruise ship.

Great! Patricia thought, watching him until he turned the corner to the elevator bank. Great—the president of Barrington Corporation thinks—make that *knows*—I'm a lovesick idiot!

Funny, the magazine article hadn't mentioned lovesick idiot as a possible explanation for her inability to ask Sam Wainwright out on a date.

A two-syllable death sentence throbbed relentlessly in Sam Wainwright's squeezed-by-tension brain.

Marriage.

Marriage.

Marriage.

He barely noticed as Patricia sat across from his desk. For all he heard, she could have been speaking in Hindu-Urdu as she reviewed the results from the second round of interviews with the graduating seniors they had met in Florida. When she opened up one file folder and then another, he was reminded of the entertainers who spin plates on top of long poles—she was just that dexterous and he was just that in awe of her. How could she keep her mind on work so well when disaster had just struck?

Marriage.

Rex Barrington II might as well have given Sam the pink slip right now.

Having picked him up off the streets and given him the chance to be somebody, Rex had one simple request before his retirement.

"I want to see the vice president of personnel married and settled down," he had said not ten minutes before. "I want to leave this company's personnel department in the hands of someone with a rock-solid personal life. This company is my baby—I don't have to worry about who's in charge when I'm relaxing on the beaches of Tahiti. But this shouldn't be a problem. You have a fiancée, right?"

Had would be more accurate, Sam thought cautiously, but before he could explain, Rex was already on to his agenda.

"Move up your wedding date."

"Sure, Rex," Sam had said, wincing as he knew it was impossible to move up a wedding date without a bride.

Rex II had a funny habit of asking, requesting, suggesting and inquiring—when what he really meant to be doing was commanding.

This was starting to sound like a command.

"I sure would love to meet the woman who has made you happy," Rex added.

So would I, Sam thought miserably.

"Bring her to the retirement party. Because if I don't see this mystery lady who's going to ensure your job performance while I'm gone, I'll just have to leave my retirement party and go find her myself."

There's a lot of women out there in the world, Sam thought.

Instead he simply agreed. "Will do, Rex."

"Remember—I want my vice president of personnel married. Married, Sam. Remember, when my son, Rex the Third, takes over when I'm gone, there'll be some corporate uncertainty. Some confusion and chaos until he finds his style of business. The vice president of personnel should be steady and stable—in your case, married."

"Sure thing, Rex."

No doubt about it. A command.

What a nightmare!

Marriage.

Marriage.

Sam.

Marriage.

Sam.

"Sam?"

Sam snapped to attention.

"What were you saying?"

Patricia tapped a pencil on his desk.

"I asked whether you think it would be appropriate for me to ask the Barrington resort managers to attend the tour of Barrington corporate headquarters for the applicants we've agreed upon," she said, pushing her reading glasses up to the bridge of her nose. She leaned forward to emphasize her point and Sam noticed the familiar, relaxing scent of vanilla and Ivory soap. "It would give the new people a chance to meet all the managers—not just the ones they'll be working with but the ones that they may fill in for in the future."

"Great idea," Sam said. He looked closely at Patricia. Efficient, reliable, weather-any-storm Patricia. If she were vice president, Rex II wouldn't ask her about marriage—there wasn't anybody who had a more stable life than Patricia. Her only weakness...chocolate. In all other areas of her life, she was as strictly disciplined as a Swiss watch.

Patricia Peel was a public television, warm milk at bedtime, brush-and-floss three times a day, cotton undies kind of woman.

Although he had never seen her underwear, hadn't even given it a thought—but if he had, they'd be cotton. Sam was sure of it.

"Sam? Are you listening to me?"

"Huh? Oh, yeah. 'ricia, hand me your glasses."

"Why?"

"They've got a little smudge on them."

She pulled them off and inspected them.

"Here. You can't see it," he said, reaching across the desk and snatching them. He pulled a tissue out of the box on the credenza behind them.

He looked at her, studying her closely. Yeah, if she was in his shoes, Rex wouldn't give a thought to whether her personal life was stable and secure. She was as sure as the Rock of Gibraltar, as on time as the birds of Capistrano and as certain as the yearly visit of Santa Claus.

She blinked back at him.

A devilish thought developed, atom by atom, in his troubled brain.

Sam had always been a problem solver. He had always been one to overcome the odds. Anyone who knew about his early life would say, in fact, that he was a never-give-up-hell-bent-for-leather kind of guy. He put the unopened aspirin bottle back in the middle drawer of his desk—this was manageable, he thought with rising confidence. He could get through this.

"Patricia, would you say that we're friends?"

She blushed scarlet and her lashes fluttered down like a curtain over her tourmaline eyes. He wondered if he had gone too far. But before he could retract his words, she jerked her head high and announced "yes" with a great deal of emphasis.

"I think we're good friends," she said, nodding vigorously. "We get along. We laugh at each other's jokes. We work together well. Yes, I would definitely say we're friends. Why do you ask?"

Sam took a mental inventory, little hearing her carefully chosen words. She was pretty, in a winsome, innocent way. But she wasn't too young—he wouldn't be thinking the thoughts he was thinking if she were too young. She could dress a little better—the gray suits she favored were more corporate than Phoenix. But when they had gone to Fort Lauderdale to recruit the incoming class of assistant managers for the Barrington resorts, he recalled her fetching, yet never vulgar, cutoffs and T-shirts. And when she had pulled her hair out of its too-tight ponytail—she had pulled a respectable share of head turns and wolf whistles at the beach.

"Patricia, do you think friends should do favors for their friends?" he asked, putting her glasses on the desk—out of her reach.

"Of course," she replied cautiously.

"Am I the kind of friend you would do a favor for?"

As soon as he asked it, he knew that was a stupid question. Of course she did favors for him. She had brought him his work and a selection of Chinese food every night for two weeks when he twisted his ankle playing baseball at the company picnic. She had joined his Thursday-night basketball team when one of the men dropped out, and she didn't play so bad. She had picked up his dry cleaning when he was too busy, and had helped plan the dinner he gave for Melissa and her family when they announced their engagement.

He tried to think if the favors he had ever done for her measured up. He had gotten her a good-size office with a view of the desert. He had persuaded Rex that she deserved the largest merit raise in the department. But he would have done that for any assistant who worked as hard as Patricia did.

The scales of friendship were clearly weighted in her favor.

"Let me ask this another way. Are you…involved with anyone?" he asked, realizing for the first time that he didn't know nearly as much about her as she did about him.

"No," she said. "I was actually going to ask you if..."

She froze, looking like a deer blinded by the headlights of an approaching car.

"You were going to ask me what?"

"Nothing," she said. "Absolutely nothing."

He was sure, at that moment, that he heard her whisper the word *wimp* or maybe it was *shrimp* or *limp*.

"What?"

"Nothing," she repeated. "Why did you ask if I was involved?"

"I wouldn't want to ask my next question if there was another man," he said cautiously.

She opened her mouth—he had never noticed how her lips were naturally the soft color of pink roses. She started to speak and then her shoulders rounded, her jewel-green eyes widening like a cat's. Her breasts strained against the architecturally starched shirt.

"What...question?"

He took a deep breath, wondering if he was making a mistake. But then that drumbeat in his head grew louder.

Marriage.

Marriage.

Marriage.

He thought of how much Rex had done for him. He thought of the poverty of his childhood, the taste of stale bread and sour milk, the smell of whiskey on his father's breath, his mother's funeral and the cheap coffin that had made him furious at his own weakness, that he, at eleven, couldn't provide something better for her last rest.

And all Rex II wanted was that his vice president of personnel be married.

"Patricia, what would you think about being my fiancée?"

Joy, so innocent and heartfelt that it could not be hidden, suffused her face, and Sam wondered if he had made a terrible, terrible mistake.

Chapter Two

"Did you just say 'fiancée'?"

Oh, great, Patricia thought. I'm sounding like a complete idiot. Of course he said fiancée.

Fiancée. Fiancée. The most beautiful French word the English language had ever borrowed.

"Was it a rhetorical question?" she added quickly. "Because if it was, I want you to know that any woman would be very blessed to be your fiancée. And as a matter of fact, when I walked into this office, I had something that I wanted to tell you that was kind of in the same subject category."

Sam blankly met her flustered gaze.

"It wasn't a rhetorical," he said.

Patricia swallowed.

"You mean, you were asking me if I wanted to be your fiancée because you want me to be your fiancée?"

Is it possible that he's felt something toward me, something he couldn't express...? She took a deep breath and suppressed a smile. No, not just a smile—a megawatt, five-alarm grin that she had to stop. Because this was a man who had just broken up with a woman and no doubt feeling lots of pain and wasn't in his right mind.

Oh, yessirree, Bob! He is in his right mind! a rebellious voice protested. He's finally noticed. Finally noticed me!

"Fiancée," Patricia repeated, not letting him off the hook even when he looked away uncomfortably. "You said you wanted me to be your fiancée. Don't you think we should take the relationship a little slower?"

He looked up sharply.

"Forget it," he said. He reached for the file folder on the top of the stack. Patricia was quicker—a proprietary hand shot out and covered Sam's. He retreated, shaking his head. "It was a thought, Patricia, a really stupid thought. My fault entirely. I shouldn't have brought it up at all. Now what were we supposed to do this morning?"

He blessed her with a boyishly wry smile, the one that made the corners of his gray eyes crinkle. A lock of light brown hair fell down his forehead and Patricia had to remind herself not to ask for his autograph because he looked handsome enough for motion pictures.

"What was the thought?" Patricia insisted, thinking it couldn't be all that stupid if it involved the word *fiancée*.

He looked out the window, to the morning heat just now slithering up from the roofs of the cars in the parking lot.

"I'm in some trouble," he said at last.

Patricia let out a breath she hadn't even known she had been holding. Trouble. Not passion. Trouble. Not awakening love. Trouble. She felt a flash of anger, feeling a little like a mouse who has been toyed with by a ferocious but disinterested cat. For any other man, the anger would have swelled— bringing with it a stern lecture and an indignant exit. But a familiar surge of affection for Sam kept her glued to her seat.

She guessed. "Does this trouble have to do with Melissa?"

"A little," he said, grimacing. "We broke up."

"I heard."

"You did?"

"I was at a baby shower for Olivia. From the legal department," she said. Sam nodded. "The woman who is handling the RSVPs for the retirement party mentioned to me that you and Melissa weren't together anymore."

Patricia left out the heartfelt conversation that had followed—how the women she had come to think of as her closest friends had giddily coached her on taking a chance, on asking him out, on making a move on the only man who had interested her in the six months she had lived in Phoenix.

"It wasn't working out," Sam said.

"So you're feeling grief?"

Sam considered this.

"No."

"Sadness?"

He shrugged inside the broad shoulders of his khaki-colored suit jacket.

"Not too much."

"You miss her?"

"Not really."

"You broke up with her?"

He nodded sheepishly.

"Is she upset?"

"Yes. She slapped me. But not very convincingly. She'll go shopping and forget this ever happened."

"Then...what's the trouble you're in?"

"Rex. Mr. Barrington."

Patricia thought of her encounter with the president and wisely decided to keep it to herself.

"Why would he be involved in this?"

Sam put his head in his hands.

"He wants to meet my fiancée. He was just in here and he asked me to introduce her to him at the retirement party."

"Tell him you've broken up."

He looked up, his normally tan and relaxed face stricken, his dove-gray eyes wide and sad.

"I didn't have the heart to do that."

Patricia could understand that. Although she herself was not close to the founder of Barrington Corporation—in fact, she was pretty sure he didn't know her name—she knew others who felt as close to him as they would their own fathers. Sam had played golf with Rex, had been invited to his home for dinner, had even worked on the same fund-raiser with Rex. And she didn't think it was just corporate ambitions that motivated Sam—he talked about Rex II with real affection.

"You're so nice to him."

"It's not niceness," Sam corrected sharply. "I'm not a nice person."

"You are."

"Don't start that again. This is the only thing we argue about. I've always told you that I'm decent— which is the minimal requirement for not being a jerk. But nice—no, I don't think so."

"I do. But let's agree to disagree on that."

"Patricia, I didn't say anything to him because of my own self-interest. He said that he was worried about leaving the personnel department in the hands of someone whose personal life isn't rock solid. As in married. So when he said he wanted me to introduce him to my fiancée, I didn't tell him that we've broken up."

"You're saying that your motivations weren't purely selfless."

"Patricia, I was completely selfish. I was thinking about my job."

"No, you weren't. You were thinking of Rex's feelings. And besides, everybody does things for a mix of reasons—some selfish, some not so selfish."

"How do you know?" he challenged. "You weren't even here when he was talking to me."

"I know you, Sam. I know that you love this job and that you'd do anything to succeed at it. But I also know that you are a kind man who is a good friend."

Sam combed his fingers through his cappuccino-colored hair.

"Sam, a good friend sometimes does strange things in the name of friendship."

He sighed heavily.

"Want to know the worst of it?" he asked, draining his coffee cup. "The first thing I thought of when you walked in was that you and I could...oh, it's too ridiculous."

"No, tell me."

"I thought you and I could go to his party as if we were engaged. You pretending that you're my fiancée, me pretending that I'm yours. I would call that pretty damned mercenary of me."

Patricia swallowed hard. This wasn't how it was supposed to be. There was supposed to be music and moonlight and Sam on his knees. He wasn't interested in her as anything but a friend. But he was in trouble—and she loved him and considered him a friend even if she wished for so much more.

A friend in trouble needing her help.

Of course, she'd do anything to help him keep the job that meant so much to him.

But her motives weren't any purer than his had

been when he had not told Rex about his broken engagement.

Because a devilish voice in her head posed a simple question.

A girl could dream, couldn't she?

And maybe turn fool's gold into a real wedding band.

"Sam, I don't think it's such a terrible idea," Patricia said, and she squelched her natural aversion to any kind of subterfuge. "In fact, I don't have an objection to doing it. I'm probably the best woman for the job of being your fiancée. We work together so closely and we spend a lot of time together even outside of nine to five. Rex would think it was quite natural that the two of us would become... involved."

Even if Sam couldn't imagine it, Patricia thought.

"Have you told Rex anything about your fiancée?" she prodded.

"No. I'm not sure I've even mentioned who she was. The woman handling the party got her number from me, but didn't pass along the name to Rex because he certainly couldn't remember it just now."

"I've heard you'd had a lot of girlfriends before you became engaged to Melissa. He probably can't keep the names straight."

Sam looked stricken.

"I'm not that much of a playboy."

Patricia impatiently tapped her pencil on her stack of files.

"Okay, okay, maybe a little bit of a playboy," Sam admitted. "But my reputation is much worse than the reality."

"And your reputation is why Rex is so interested in seeing you married and settled down."

Sam abruptly stood up, and Patricia wondered if she had gone too far.

"It's ridiculous," he said, pacing the soft red Navaho rug. "I should march right into his office and tell him that I broke up with my fiancée two days ago and he can do with that information what he chooses."

"And break his heart."

Sam stopped dead in his tracks.

They both knew Patricia was right. It would break Rex's heart. He liked to know his employees were happy, and he fretted over every one of them.

"Besides, you can't do this," Sam said. "You're too young."

"I'm twenty-nine."

"I'm not talking about years."

"Well, I think I can judge whether I'm old enough."

"Why would you want to do it?" Sam asked with just a trace of suspicion. "If you think your job's on the line, you're absolutely wrong. It's mine. In fact, if I lost my job this morning, they'd be nailing your nameplate to the door of this office by noon."

"I know that."

"You could be vice president."

"No, thanks."

"Why would you want to do this for me?"

"I'm your friend, remember?" Patricia asked. "And we're talking about being engaged for a few weeks at most. When Rex is on his world tour after the retirement party, we'll quietly announce that we've broken up. When he's on a beach in Tahiti, your marriage plans are not going to be his top priority. And with the new boss coming in…"

"Oh, yeah," Sam said.

Nobody at Barrington needed to be reminded that Rex II's mysterious son, Rex III, would be moving into the president's office—and job insecurity was high.

Patricia pressed her point.

"With Rex the Third coming in, it probably would look good for both of us to look like we're stable, loyal members of the Barrington team."

"But we are."

"I know that. You know that. But neither one of us has met the Third. He doesn't know anything about us that his father doesn't tell him. And if his father tells him how pleased he is with you—and me—both our jobs will be secure."

Sam sat down at the desk.

"So we're engaged," he said.

Patricia nodded uncertainly.

"Yes, I suppose we are. Now we are. Officially."

He reached across the desk and shook her hand. "Congratulations."

"You're supposed to offer me best wishes," Patricia corrected, snatching her glasses from his desk.

"The groom-to-be gets congratulated because he has won the prize of the woman's heart. The bride-to-be is offered best wishes because marriage is supposed to be a more difficult enterprise for women than men."

"Gotcha," Sam said, pulling the stack of file folders towards him. "All right, let's take a look at the first one here. Oh, by the way, what'd you have for breakfast?"

"Granola and a diet cola. I always do."

"Sounds easy to remember. What do you sleep in?"

"I beg your pardon?"

"What do you wear to bed?"

Patricia opened her mouth. Closed it. Opened it again. Closed it again. She was sure she looked like a fish.

There was no way she was going to confess to an extralarge Tweety Bird T-shirt with a frayed hem. She was trying to come up with what a sophisticated woman might wear—Chanel No. 5 and nothing else?—when Sam shook his head.

"Patricia, I'd know these things if I were your man."

Just the way he said "your man" was enough to put a flame-hot blush on her face.

"You know, a woman could get hurt in a setup like this," Sam said. "A man, too, for that matter. If there were any misunderstandings."

"I don't misunderstand a thing," Patricia said defensively. "This is just a business thing. And we're pretty clear about the limits."

"For instance, no sex. I wouldn't want you to think of me as unprofessional—although heaven knows this is the most unprofessional thing I've ever asked my assistant to do."

"Good idea. No sex," she agreed, actually feeling relieved. Sex was an unknown, and putting it off-limits made this engagement easier on her than…well, than a real engagement would be.

"A friendship could get hurt," Sam continued, "if one of us were inexperienced and had expectations. And I wouldn't want you hurt."

She brought her shoulders back and raised her head high.

"I am not inexperienced."

"Oh, really?"

"Sam Wainwright, we've never talked about my love life, but I have a lot more going for me than you'd think. You'd be very surprised."

She crossed her fingers in her lap.

"I didn't say you didn't have any men in your life. I was just asking."

"Well, you've asked and I've answered. I'm experienced…enough."

"And your expectations?"

"None," she said, which was strictly true. The reality was that she didn't expect him to notice her.

But he hadn't asked her about hopes and dreams and wishes.

"And I wear silk to bed every night. Wipe that look of disbelief off your face."

She dared him to challenge her. He studied her, the full panoply of emotions from puzzlement to bafflement to confusion crossing his features.

"I think there must be a lot about you I don't know," he said at last. "Silk, huh?"

"Yes. You were thinking I'm a cotton nightgown kind of woman."

"Flannel would have been my first guess."

"Silk. Red silk. Yes, red. Bright red." And before he could follow that up, she fired off her own salvo. "What do you wear to bed?"

Sam shrugged.

"Nothin'," he said. "Nothin' at all."

The mental picture that came to Patricia's mind was sharp, clear and way too vivid.

"Oh!" she exclaimed. And then, before he could say another word, she shoved her glasses on her face and flipped open her notebook filled with her evaluations of the job candidates. "Enough personal stuff. Shall we think about the assistant manager for the Vail facility?"

Chapter Three

"I think that wraps things up," Sam said at the end of the hour. "You've picked some strong candidates. You always do."

"Thank you," Patricia said, pulling the files together in a neat stack. "About that other matter..."

Sam looked up from his paperwork.

"You don't have to do it if you've reconsidered."

"No, I haven't reconsidered. It's just I don't even know where to begin with questions for you. Sam, I know a lot about your professional life, and I now know that you wear..."

"Nothing to bed," Sam prompted.

"Nothing to bed. But at the party, Rex could very well ask me some questions I wouldn't know the answers to. Maybe we should work this all out. Not during business hours, of course."

It wasn't asking him out for a date.

But it still took a lot of gumption.

"Let's have dinner tonight," Sam suggested.

"Meet you in the break room, say around six?"

At least four times a month they ate dinner together in the break room when work kept them late. Sometimes they'd order in Chinese food or a pizza. That was if Patricia remembered to take care of it. When Sam was in charge of dinner, it was chips, candy and a can of pop from the vending machine. He always sprung for the quarters, but Patricia always felt guilty afterward—all that salt, sugar and empty calories.

Sam shook his head.

"Dehlia's," he said, naming the swankiest restaurant in Phoenix. "If you're my fiancée, you'd be familiar with it. Melissa sure was. Oh, and by the way, here's this. I've had this in my pocket for two days. I keep looking at it, wondering what I'm doing wrong in life."

He reached into his shirt pocket and pulled out a ring with a pear-shape—heck, pear-size—diamond. A familiar ring—Patricia had helped him pick it out after Melissa had rejected his first choice. Melissa had insisted that four carats was an absolute minimum, that anything less would signal to others that he did not respect her. Patricia had wondered why Sam hadn't given Melissa the boot then and there.

But no, he had asked Patricia to come with him during a Wednesday lunch hour to see a breathtaking array of gems at James Little Jewelers. The respect and attention the jeweler gave to Sam led Patricia to believe Melissa was a regular customer. Or that Sam was.

Patricia looked at the ring he held out to her. It threw the morning sunlight out in quick brush strokes of color.

"It's too big."

"I know," Sam said. "I always thought it screamed money instead of saying anything about love. But would you wear it?"

"As long as you don't get mad if I accidentally blind you with it."

She took the ring and put it on her left ring finger. The ring was heavy and clumsy on her hand. Unexpectedly she felt melancholy. It isn't supposed to be like this, she thought.

An engagement to fool other people was wrong; it was playing with something sacred.

Somebody was going to get hurt.

And it would most likely be her.

"The ring's not you," Sam said, clearly misinterpreting her sudden change of mood. "Want me to get you another one?"

Patricia shook her head.

"This is only for a few weeks," she said. "And I'll return it in a suitable huff when we break up."

He smiled, in just that way he had—a little more on the left side than the right. With a mischievous twinkle in his dark eyes. As always, provoking her heart to flip-flop—*thaddump, thaddump*—like a fresh-caught fish at the bottom of a boat.

"Thanks," he said, rubbing his jaw. "Just don't slap me as hard as Melissa did."

"Promise."

She gathered up her file folders and notepad. Just as she reached the door, he called her name.

"I'm not really good at saying things about emotions," he said. "But thank you. You're a real friend."

He seemed about to say more, but then he cleared his throat.

"See you at Dehlia's at eight."

Patricia shrugged a reasonable facsimile of goodbye and hustled down the terra-cotta-tiled hallway. When she got to her office, she threw down the files and slammed the door for privacy.

Friend.

That's what she was. Nothing more. Six months she had been in this office—and Sam would never, ever look at her with the eyes of a lover. She had to keep this in mind—she was a friend doing another friend a favor.

Friend.

And yet, all the force of reality and sensible thinking couldn't completely squelch her hope. As tender and fragile as a desert bloom and as determined to survive without water or encouragement. He'd see her at dinner, he'd look across the table, he'd realize that he had been a fool for six solid months...

"I've got to get out more," she said quietly, pulling off her suit jacket. Although the Barrington offices were air-conditioned, her white cotton blouse was damp with sweat. She tugged at the three covered buttons at its collar.

She had to go on those blind dates that her office friends kept trying to set up. She had to stop dreaming about Sam every night. She had to discipline herself not to think about him every waking minute. She had to join the singles group at her church. She had to meet those men her mother kept sending over from France. She had to forget about him....

And she would, somehow.

After they broke up, she thought, looking down at the brilliant diamond on her hand.

"Sorry I'm late," Patricia apologized, closing the door behind her. The women at the round Formica-topped table turned around to greet her. One sky-blue plastic chair had been reserved for her. Since August in Phoenix is as close to the blazes of Hades as anybody should ever get, the women ate indoors...and stuck the thermostat on sixty-five although the room never got any cooler than eighty. Patricia thought the lunchroom was particularly stifling today. She took off her jacket, slid into her seat and gave everyone a shy smile. "I had some paperwork."

"Anything about the Third?" Sophia asked, tossing her curly blond hair as if the query was merely casual chitchat.

They all knew she was determined to marry the mysterious son of Rex II, the son who was taking over Barrington in just another week. No one had seen him—not even Sophia who had become his personal assistant. "Any information at all?"

"No, but what about Mike?" Patricia asked. She opened her lunch bag. She slid the homemade brownie in front of Olivia, who had developed quite a sweet tooth during her pregnancy. "Mike from the mail room is awfully cute."

"No way. He's not doing anything with his life and I want to do something with mine. I want a house and kids and a husband. Someone with some ambition and charm and family interests."

"Someone like the Third?" teased Rachel, the diminutive brunette from Accounting.

As the women laughed, Sophia shook her finger at Rachel.

"You mark my words, I'm going to have Rex the Third's ring on my hand in six months," she said confidently.

"Speaking of hands, would you get a load of this," Olivia said, grasping Patricia's. "It's gotta be four carats."

"Four point five," Patricia said gently, steadying her hand by placing it flat on the table. The women leaned over their sandwiches and salads.

"Wow," said Sophia.

"Cubic zirconia?" asked Molly, a copywriter from the advertising department. "I heard they had a sale on costume jewelry at the mall."

"No, it's a diamond," Patricia said.

There was a collective gasp.

"I didn't know they made diamonds that big for

regular people," Rachel said. "I mean—not royalty or movie stars."

Patricia struggled to keep her whole arm from shaking while the women oohed and aahed. She was about to lie to her friends. She hated this part, but she had spent twenty minutes in her office practicing how she would do it.

There had been no paperwork keeping her busy— it had been rehearsal time.

And it was now opening night.

She had her audience's attention.

"I've got something to tell you."

The five women at the table fell silent, mouths open and eyes totally focused on her. She wasn't used to that kind of attention. She licked her dry lips.

"I'm engaged."

The stillness was terrifying. Could they tell she was lying? Would they be mad at her? Would they not be her friends anymore? Would they make her take her lunch elsewhere?

Olivia shrieked. So loud that Patricia worried she was in labor. But no, those were joyful sounds. And she threw her arms around Patricia and gave her as much of a hug as her expanding belly permitted. All around the table, the women reached out to touch Patricia and to offer her their best wishes.

"This is so wonderful!" Rachel gushed.

"Who's the lucky guy?" Sophia demanded.

"Yeah, that's right!" Olivia said, pulling out of her embrace to regard Patricia somberly. "You never date because you're always thinking about Sam. And he's a playboy, except now that he's engaged... Wait a minute, he broke up with Melissa, didn't he?''

Patricia nodded, not trusting herself with words.

"He did it because he figured out he loved you and not her?" Rachel squealed.

Patricia opened her mouth to say, yes. But then she paused—these friends would not be fooled. They knew she had despaired of ever getting Sam's attention and, until this past weekend, had accepted that Melissa was going to have the honor of being called Mrs. Sam Wainwright.

Rex II will meet me at the retirement party and think we've been engaged for a while.

These women know better.

At dinner, I'd better tell Sam about the time discrepancy, Patricia thought.

Meanwhile, she had an edge-of-their-seats audience wanting the full scoop on her romance.

"Yes, as a matter of fact that's what happened," she said at last. They didn't budge. No one suggested changing the topic. No one even followed up with a question, because a friend was honor bound to spill all the beans at this point. She took a deep breath. "Remember when I said that I was going to try and, well, you know..."

"No, I don't know," Sophia said. "What did you do to him?"

"Seduce," Olivia prompted. "That's the word

you're looking for. You prim little maiden. You obviously did a good job of seduction."

"Seduce," Patricia said, worrying the collar of her blouse. She wouldn't have the slightest clue how to seduce a man, but none of these women would know that. "Yes, that's what I did."

"You seduced Sam Wainwright?" Rachel demanded. "In his office? During business hours? Weren't you worried about someone walking in?"

"We didn't actually...do anything there."

"Nothing?"

"We kissed, of course," Patricia said.

"Of course," Olivia agreed.

"Yeah, but you have a ring on your finger," Cindy pointed. Cindy was planning her own wedding to her boss in the New Product Division. She had had her own romance come true and was genuinely delighted to see Patricia's happiness. "That's enough for me. I don't care what you did in his office, you little hussy, you."

The affectionate twinkle in her eye confirmed her "Go, girl!" attitude.

"More power to you," Rachel said. "What'd he say when you told him you were interested in him?"

"That's assuming they talked," Olivia said. "It could have been a marathon kiss."

I never got a chance to kiss him or to tell him how I felt, Patricia thought. But she plowed ahead with her story.

"I told him I had always been attracted to him."

"That's putting it mildly," Sophia interjected and was promptly shushed by the rest of the table.

"And that's when he told me that he had always felt the same way," Patricia said, while her brain chanted fantasy, fantasy, fantasy. "And then he just...kissed me."

"And asked you to marry him," Sophia finished. She shook her head and sighed. "That's incredible. And so romantic. I wonder if it'll be like that with me and Rex the Third."

"Would you stop talking about him?" Cindy demanded. "We're concentrating on Patricia."

"Sorry, Patricia," Sophia said. "I didn't mean to change the topic."

Patricia would have been happy enough to talk about the Third.

"I'm a little baffled here," Olivia said, breaking apart the brownie. "We know he broke up last week with Melissa. And then this morning you came to his office and all you said was..."

"Stop it, Olivia," Rachel said. "You're sounding like a lawyer cross-examining a witness."

"But I *am* a lawyer."

"Well, can it. Because this is romance we're talking about," Rachel said. "I think we need to plan a bridal shower. What do you say, girls?"

"No, really, that's okay," Patricia said, panic swelling as her friends started talking all at once. She hadn't considered this possibility. "You're awfully nice, but I don't need one. Really I don't."

"Why wouldn't you?" Olivia asked. She bit into

the brownie. "I mean, is there a problem you're not telling us about?"

"No, of course not," Patricia said. "I'd be delighted."

"Let's have it at my house," Cindy said.

"No, mine," Rachel countered.

As a good-natured argument erupted, Patricia quietly pulled her sandwich out of its plastic wrap. She didn't feel much like eating. It was getting so complicated. A simple favor for Sam was turning into a web of deception. She started to push away her food and noticed Olivia looking at her.

Could Olivia tell she was lying to them?

"If you're not going to eat that sandwich, can I have it?" Olivia asked. "I swear you make the best chicken salad in Arizona."

"Sure," Patricia said. "I'm too excited to eat."

"I got that way before my wedding, too," Olivia said. "I'm so happy for you. It's what you've always wanted."

Patricia looked around the table. The five women had let her enter their circle of friendship. They cared about her. They were planning a bridal shower for her.

How would she ever explain to them that she had lied about her happiness in order to give Sam his?

Chapter Four

When business travel took Patricia to hotels, spas and restaurants that competed with the Barrington Corporation's holdings, Patricia usually paid close attention to details—sometimes even jotting down notes.

But as she edged her blue hatchback up the palm-lined drive to Dehlia's, Patricia felt not a smidgen of professional interest in the strong, lean lines of the architecture or the smart salute of the doorman waiting to greet her.

She didn't have the slightest urge to take the spiral-bound notebook from her briefcase and write down "valet parking attendants wear bright red bow ties" or "good location with view of desert sunset."

Instead, she felt a sense of awe, coupled with a sinking feeling that she had made a terrible error in judgment. Oh, not in getting engaged to Sam. She had successfully persuaded the girls to put off a bridal shower for at least a month, and she knew that she would explain everything to them the week after Rex II left. She didn't count on forgiveness but she did count on their essential goodness. Her mother, thanks to the diplomatic corps, was far away in Paris and would never know—a good thing since Mrs. Peel's advice was exactly the sort of thing Patricia generally avoided. Patricia would like her life to be less...exciting than that of her mother.

This engagement was a great idea—if nothing else, she'd get to see a side of Sam that he generally kept well hidden. The what-does-he-want-in-a-woman-and-not-in-an-employee side.

But, her spirits faltered when she saw the crowd gathering outside the heavy mesquite door of the restaurant. Phoenix snowbirds are long gone by August and year-rounders who can't get out of town are accustomed to quick service and a generally casual atmosphere.

Nix to both at Dehlia's.

"Sam likes glamour," she muttered. "If these women are any indication, Sam's a regular sequins/miniskirt/big hair junkie."

She looked down at her gray suit, a little wilted in the late-afternoon heat. Her shoes, black pumps that had seemed sensible yet sophisticated in the store, now looked downright orthopedic. She got out of her car, half expecting the valet to ask if she needed a walker. Then she remembered her briefcase before locking the door and scanned the curb for any sign of Sam.

"Miss, I need your key!" the valet said.

"Oh, sorry," Patricia said. It took her several nail-splitting minutes to extract her car key from her key ring.

"First time?" the valet asked gently.

At everything, yes, Patricia thought.

"Here, I got the key out," she said. "I'm meeting my...fiancé."

Not a flicker of curiosity crossed his face as he handed her a ticket to retrieve her car. All right, Patricia thought, total strangers can be fooled into thinking that I'm engaged.

"Go to the head of the line and give your name to the maitre d'," the valet advised and, without a backward glance, he shoved his fingers into his mouth and whistled a stop warning to an approaching car.

Adjusting the shoulder strap on her briefcase, she squeezed through a well-dressed, well-coifed see-and-be-seen line.

Just inside the door, a small man with the face of a bulldog and a crisply sheered dark suit acknowledged her with a sharp nod.

"Would *señora* care for me to take her briefcase?" he asked with a precise Castillian accent.

"No, thanks," Patricia said, staring over his shoulder into the spacious, airy dining room bathed in turquoise, Guatemalan red and Pueblo gold tones.

"I'm meeting someone here. My fiancé. Sam Wainwright."

A barely there jowl wiggle was the only sign of the maitre d's doubt.

"Mr. Wainwright has a standing reservation for two but he has not yet arrived," the maitre d' said. "Would you care to have a seat at the... Oh, Mr. Wainwright, how very nice to see you."

"Dino, it's a pleasure," Sam said, coming up behind Patricia. He had changed into a European cut midnight blue suit with a white silk shirt. He smelled fresh and citrusy and his hair was shower-damp. "You have my usual table?"

Dino bowed.

"But of course. This young lady indicates that she is your..." He rubbed his fingers together as if the nuances of the English language were a mystery.

"My fiancée," Sam supplied. He kissed Patricia chastely on the cheek. The touch was startling—to Patricia and Dino!

The maitre d's lips puckered around an especially sour taste.

"But what about...?" Dino reconsidered his question and solemnly said, "Bravo. I offer you my congratulations."

He briskly stacked two leather-bound menus and a wine list and led them to a button-tufted leather banquette overlooking the twinkling, glittering, neon-splattered downtown Phoenix. And beyond that, the mountains with the pale pink reminder of the sunset.

"Enjoy your dinner," Dino said, and before withdrawing he sniffed loudly.

"He's used to seeing Melissa," Patricia guessed.

"Melissa and I came here every week," Sam confirmed, taking a sip from his water glass. "Her grandfather was the Stanhope that first discovered the silver and tin on the Chulla Canyon. When the seam was cleared out a generation later, Melissa's father discovered real-estate development could make even more money than metals. Melissa is used to the finer things in life, including this restaurant."

"Bet she didn't come here in a gray suit, carrying a briefcase."

"No, but that's because she didn't have a job. Although she did seem to make a career out of flying to New York to see her favorite designers. Hey, you're not feeling out of place, are you?"

"Of course not," Patricia bristled. "But look at the women at the other tables."

Sam took a quick, discreet look around the crowded dining room. Then he looked at Patricia. Under his scrutiny, she shoved her bitten-to-the-quick nails under the heavy damask tablecloth.

"The usual crowd."

"And me?"

"You look like you always do."

"Boring."

"No, you're just a more…dependable person than the regulars here."

A woman in a pale green leather miniskirt and

white patent leather boots passed their table. Patricia caught herself watching Sam's appraisal.

Dependable, she thought. *Yuck.*

"Don't underestimate dependable," he said, turning his attention to her. "In fact, in a room filled with teased and perfumed and sequined ladies, it's nice to have someone looking so natural."

He reached across the table and flicked a stray lock of hair behind her ears.

"Natural" sounded like the Miss Congeniality Award at a beauty pageant. At the end of the evening, nobody ever remembered who was the most dependable friend or even where she came from. They only remembered the girl with the crown and the roses, and Patricia was going to do everything in her power to win her own title—Mrs. Sam Wainwright!

"If a new dress or a new hairdo will make you feel more comfortable, let's do it," Sam said. "Tomorrow, let's take off a little early. I'll take you shopping. My treat. All right?"

"I don't want you to buy me things," Patricia insisted.

"I know. Jeez, Patricia, you could learn from Melissa."

"Oh, really?"

"Mew a little. Pout. Toss your head just so. Insist that life's not worth living unless you have that newest little number by Isaac Mizrahi. Tell me you'll be sooooo happy if I get it for you."

"I don't need you to buy me a dress. I just think

I should get one—at least for the party. And maybe a haircut. I mean, style."

"You didn't pay attention to that lesson."

"I don't want to learn. Didn't you hate that?"

"I didn't notice it too much. She really wasn't that bad. It was how she was taught. You aren't like that. Anything I can do to make this engagement easier on you, I want to do it. Besides, you'll want me to approve of your new dress for the retirement party."

"I will?"

"Yeah, because it's black tie. You're better at picking out..." He caught the end of his sentence and reconsidered.

"Gray suits," Patricia prompted.

He put his head in his hands, confirming for Patricia everything she thought about her appearance.

"It's okay, Sam, I know my limits. Why don't we buy a dress together?"

He squeezed her hand and she smiled weakly.

She had a little more than a week to change Sam's mind, to make him give her a longer look. And she was going to use her time wisely.

"Now let's work out some more important items," he announced.

"Like what?"

"Like what you're having for dinner," Sam said, opening her menu before her. "The menu is in Spanish and the street Spanish I know isn't adequate. But whenever I say 'porterhouse steak,' the waiter understands me. Maybe you'll have better luck.''

When the waiter came to the table, he announced that the maitre d' had sent them a complimentary bottle of champagne to celebrate their engagement.

"I'll have what he's having," she said when Sam was done ordering.

When the waiter murmured his approval of Patricia's selections and withdrew from the table, Sam gently touched his fluted glass to hers.

"Thank you so much," he said. "To friends."

She put down her glass. Playtime was over. Recess was called on account of having to get down to business.

"You have a lot to tell me," she said.

"Ladies first."

"Age before beauty."

"Ha! You're more interesting."

"Hardly. And besides, I'm not the one wanting to be engaged."

"All right, you win. I'm thirty-six years old."

"Knew that."

"I grew up in the rough side of Phoenix."

"Kind of knew that, too."

"My mother died when I was eleven."

"I'm sorry, but you told me about that."

"And my father is…I don't even know where he is."

Patricia looked away. She knew it was a painful subject for Sam.

"I went to the University of Arizona on a basketball scholarship,'' Sam continued. ''But spent most of the time on the bench because there were better players. I didn't care because I wasn't there to become a pro, I was there to get an education.''

''I don't know how good the other players were but I knew all that.''

''Now you know so much about my life, let's do yours. Twenty-nine.''

''Got that from my personnel record.''

''Your parents were career diplomats. Your father died in Bhutan. Your mother is now an attaché to the French ambassador in Paris.''

''Got it in one guess.''

''You went to a boarding school in London, then one in Sweden.''

''Switzerland.''

''I knew it began with an *S*. And you went to Northwestern University in Chicago.''

''Ho-hum.''

''And after eight years working at the University Club of Chicago, you came to Barrington.''

They each drank from their glasses.

''So that's it,'' Patricia concluded. ''We know a lot of general stuff about each other. We've been friends. We tell each other things.''

''If we were lovers, we'd tell each other more.''

''How much more?'' Patricia asked, draining her glass. She leaned back to give the waiter room to present her first course. The fragrant risotto reminded her she hadn't eaten since noon. That must account for the light-headedness she felt.

"Lovers. Past lovers."

He nodded at the waiter, who twisted the pepper shaker over his rice. Patricia declined just so that the waiter would get out of earshot.

Lovers?

Hadn't had any, Patricia thought to herself.

"I'll go first," Sam said.

"I won't have to talk for the rest of the evening if we get started with you."

He playfully snapped his napkin at her.

"I'm not as much of a playboy as you think. I can't figure out why I have this reputation."

"It's because you're so handsome," Patricia blurted out. Oh, great, she thought, why don't you just tell him that he's the man you dream about at night?

"So handsome?" he asked, looking genuinely baffled.

"Everyone thinks so," she said, covering up her own particular opinion on the subject. "And a handsome man is just assumed to be...busy."

He opened his mouth, looking at her intently—so intently that Patricia was sure that he would ask her what she assumed. What she thought. Whether she thought he was handsome.

And then she'd just have to hope that the entire Sonoran Desert opened up and swallowed her.

"Do you think I'm handsome?"

"You're okay," she said with a nonchalant shrug.

"Do you think I'm a playboy?"

"A little."

"Then there's the truth," he said at last.

"Why don't you tell me the truth?"

"I had a few—honestly, we'd call them one-night stands—when I was in college and for the couple of years after graduation. I'm not proud of that, but you should know. Or, actually, you would know if we were really...getting married. Then I had a two-year relationship with an actress who lived in Scottsdale. I went out with a model from New York, but I spent more time in airports than actually with her. And I met Melissa at a charity ball two years ago and... Aren't you hungry?"

Patricia looked down at her untouched plate.

"I'm just trying to pay attention."

"It's your turn."

How could she tell him? What would he think of her? When she had been twenty, being a virgin seemed okay. She had been bounced around too much as a teen to develop any relationships, and college had been hard work—or maybe it was just that it was more comfortable spending Friday nights in the library or out with girlfriends than at the singles bars that cluttered the neighborhood around campus. When she was twenty-five, she had several relationships behind her—but none that had blossomed into the all-consuming love she thought should be lovemaking's prerequisite.

But after twenty-five, when one young man had called her a prude and a freak because she wouldn't sleep with him, she had started to wonder about herself.

It wasn't something she thought about frequently, but it was there. Somehow she knew that Sam would treat this "problem" of hers seriously, but she also sensed that Sam would think her more fragile than she figured herself to be. He might even think her too fragile to enter into this deception.

"Should I send back your risotto?" he asked.

"Oh, no," Patricia said, rousing herself abruptly from her thoughts. "Let's see, there was Belmondo. He was the ski instructor at the boarding school in Lausane, Switzerland. I was eighteen."

There actually was a Belmondo. He really was a ski instructor. And Patricia really had been eighteen. But the way her words lingered between her and Sam left a lot of room for speculation.

"But the relationship didn't last when I moved back to America for college."

Of course it didn't last. There wasn't anything to last. Belmondo was forty-eight years old, had a wife and three children and wouldn't have remembered Patricia's name—much less what she looked like— since he had over a hundred students each semester.

"Then there was Steve—he was in the same business class at Northwestern," Patricia continued. "We pretty much kept up our relationship until I moved to Barrington."

Steve had taken a job at the University Club's personnel department just as she had. And his partner, a dapper wedding planner from the north side of the city, had often told Patricia that he'd find her a husband. Of course, he hadn't—but he tried his best to set up blind dates with nearly every groom's best man.

"Okay, Belmondo and Steve," Sam said. "I think I can keep that straight."

Patricia relaxed. She even tried a bite of the lightly spiced risotto. She was starting to relax. This was going to work out just fine. She'd go to the party with Sam. Rex would ask them a few polite questions, there might have to be some deception, but Sam would keep his job. She would have done a favor for a friend, and she might, just might, get his attention.

One week to turn his head around. She could do it. She could do it if she set her mind to it.

She wasn't nervous anymore. Her face, which had felt hot and red, was now cool and refreshed. The food, which before had made her stomach do flip-flops, was every bit as delicious as advertised.

The champagne was wonderful, she was with the man of her dreams. Life was all right.

She smiled as Sam refilled her glass.

And then he asked the lethal question.

"So when did we first know it was love?"

Chapter Five

Patricia's fork clattered as it hit her plate. Although Dehlia's was quickly filling up and the noise level was outpacing the delicate classical guitar music, several diners at nearby tables glanced over at the disturbance.

Patricia gulped at her champagne, and the bubbles, so sweet, did not comfort her or give her confidence.

It was a startling question—one she could answer honestly by saying, "I started thinking about you the first moment I met you, but firm denial kept me from realizing I was head over heels, hopelessly forever in love with you for at least another month. But from there on out, I've pretty much been doomed to love you."

Or perhaps "I couldn't stop thinking about you after you interviewed me for the position, and when

I was offered a better job at the St. Louis Ritz-Carlton, and the University Club of Chicago even offered to meet and beat your offer so that I'd stay, I still had to take your job. And when I drove my rental truck down from Chicago, all I could do was pray you weren't married.''

Or perhaps ''I work next to you every day and I really feel honored that you consider me a friend. But I'm a wimp who can't ask you out even though I practice all the time—of course I wouldn't when you were engaged—and I think asking you out for a date scares me more than bungee jumping, sky-diving and the movie *Psycho* all rolled into one.''

But honesty would only baffle Sam—and embarrass herself. She chose her words carefully, just like she always chose her words when they were discussing...business.

''I think we should play up the fact that we haven't made our relationship public because we wanted to maintain not merely the appearance but the reality of professionalism.''

''That doesn't sound very romantic.''

''It's not meant to sound romantic. It's meant to answer the question.''

''I think if someone asks me, I'll say that I've worked with you, gone on business trips with you, even considered you a good after-hours friend,'' Sam said. ''But nothing more. Until one day, I took a good look at you. A real good look. And I realized that underneath those sensible gray suits beat the heart of a sensuous and vibrant woman who drives me wild with desire. Or maybe you could be the one to have taken a good look at me."

They stared at each other. For an instant, Patricia wondered if maybe he *was* looking at her. Looking at her in that "real good look" way. Patricia took a deep breath, bit her lower lip, forced herself to meet—and keep—his gaze.

"Maintain not merely the appearance but the…what did you say?" Sam asked.

She let out her breath.

"Reality of professionalism."

"Right. Your idea sounds better."

"More realistic, too," she added.

"What about those women at Olivia's shower?" Sam asked. "They knew I had broken up with Melissa. They've got to know that we haven't been engaged all this time. And if Rex ever compares notes with those ladies…"

"That's what I was worried about, but I don't think it'll ever happen," Patricia insisted. "Nobody ever met Melissa except me. And I only did because my office is two doors down from yours."

"And because she once gave you her car keys and told you to go out to the parking lot and start her air-conditioning because the heat would ruin her hair."

"Now I remember."

"I've always assumed that your ignorance about how to get the air conditioner to work was intentional."

Patricia bit her lip.

It wasn't anything she'd have admitted to while he was engaged to Melissa....

They both laughed at the memory.

"Point is, no one knows Melissa by sight," Patricia continued. "They only know that a woman named Melissa existed. That she was listed as your guest for the party and now she's not."

"That's bad enough."

"I've been giving this some thought this afternoon. I have a plan."

"Your plans are always good."

"All you have to do is say Melissa was a code name for me. So when the office gossips heard you talking about going out with Melissa, you were actually talking about me."

"Good idea. Thank God her family was so opposed to her marrying me that they never officially announced the engagement. Otherwise, our pictures would have ended up in the society page and Mildred Van Hess would know."

"Why would Rex's assistant know about the Stanhope family?"

"She reads the society page every day," Sam said. "Whenever I go into Rex's office, she has some new tidbit about which Hollywood starlet is buying a condo in Phoenix and which business leader is getting married. I never talked about Melissa with her—now I'm glad I didn't."

"But she would know the Stanhope name?"

"Absolutely. On any Monday morning, she'll be

able to tell you which of the best Phoenix families had a good weekend and which ones didn't.''

''Then I guess it is good Melissa's family wouldn't officially announce the engagement. Why didn't they?''

''Because they thought I was social climbing.''

''You're just as good as Melissa!'' Patricia cried out indignantly. She ducked her head as a woman seated at the next table stared blankly.

''Patricia, I grew up in a shack made out of corrugated steel and two-by-fours,'' he said gently, although the tension in his face made it clear that the memory of his early years stung. ''My mother considered it a move up when we got a trailer. My father ran off when I was little and my mother died when I was eleven. I started with nothing and the Stanhope family was always concerned that I'd end up with nothing. Or worse, that they'd have to bail Melissa out of a disastrous marriage.''

She felt his anger and humiliation radiate at the memory.

''You're better than them.''

''You're a good friend to think so. And you're already a better fiancée than Melissa.''

Friend. Fiancée. Friend. Fiancée.

He had no idea how the words affected her. And how she was going to change how he felt about those words...and about her!

The busboy cleared away their plates just as the waiter rolled a butler's tray to their table.

"Enjoy your dinner," he said, as he proudly presented their plates.

"So tomorrow let's take the afternoon off," Sam said, cutting into his steak. "We'll find you a dress for the party. And you said you wanted a haircut? How 'bout a manicure, too?"

Patricia looked down at her bitten-to-the-quick nails.

"I don't think it would do much good. But I'd better do it—because these don't look so good."

"Oh, Patricia, you have no idea how nice you are," he said, tousling her hair. He didn't notice how she winced at the word *nice*. "But if this stuff will make you more comfortable in your role as my fiancée, I want you to do it. My treat. Unless you have a regular salon you use, I'll call Gascon tonight and tell him to fit you in tomorrow afternoon."

"Gascon?"

"He owns Gascon Salon, the best in Phoenix. He's usually booked months in advance, but he grew up in my neighborhood. We played basketball together. He'll fit you in. We'll go right after lunch. We just have to finish reviewing those files, don't we?"

"Yes. There's only about ten to go."

Within minutes, they were hotly debating the merits of the many college students who hoped to work for Barrington Corporation when they graduated.

The busy valet was grateful when Patricia said she'd just as soon get her own car as wait in line.

Escorting Patricia to her car, Sam was aware of how Patricia walked just slightly ahead of him and kept a distance between them that was comfortable for a long-standing friendship.

Buddy distance, but not intimate.

A couple walking nearby put their arms around each other. The woman's head rested on her man's shoulder.

"Patricia, we've got one other problem."

She produced her key chain from the bottom of her purse and struggled to slip her car key back onto it.

"What problem?"

"I know we said no sex. But we have to be able to…touch."

She looked as startled as if he had announced they were going to suck each other's blood. Didn't do a lot for a man's ego.

"Touch… How?"

"Well, I know we just put together that seminar for the managers about how they shouldn't put their arms around their staff or make comments about their appearance or in any way suggest…"

"That's sexual harassment."

"Well, I'm always watching myself to make sure I don't cross over any lines of professional behavior."

"You never do."

"But I just realized this isn't going to work unless

I can dip over that line a little bit—at least at the party.''

"I see what you mean.''

"All I'm talking about is holding hands or putting my arm around you,'' Sam continued. Gee, the look on her face was enough to make any man feel unsure of himself. "Maybe even a kiss. It won't be terrible, I promise.''

He couldn't make out her features—she turned away from the glare of the streetlight just as he thought he saw a blush emerge on her cheeks.

"I suppose it won't be as bad as dissecting frogs in eighth-grade science.''

"Thanks, Patricia.''

"What do you have in mind?''

"How did Belmondo hold your hand?''

She looked at him blankly.

"Belmondo?''

"The skiing instructor.''

"Oh, yeah! I forgot who he was for a moment.''

Sam wondered if there were so many men in her life that she couldn't remember them all...perhaps her freckle-faced innocence wasn't true to herself.

"We just...held hands like everyone else, I guess.''

Sam took her hand, entwining his fingers through hers, careful to not squeeze too hard. Her fingers were so delicate and small. And one of her nails scraped gently against his palm.

"Like this?'' he asked.

She kept her gaze firmly pinned on a window

across the street. What could possibly be so interesting about the grocery store?

"And what about kissing Belmondo?"

She glared at him.

"I would never think of...I mean, of course we did. Kissed all the time. Every opportunity we got."

"Could I kiss you?"

"Now?"

"No, I'd like to make an appointment."

"Okay, okay, you can kiss me."

"Just for practice. If we get into a situation where we need it, I don't want to be too awkward."

For the first time in his life, he was worried about awkwardness with a woman!

"Okay, go ahead," she said breathlessly.

She closed her eyes, raising her face upward.

Sam stared.

He didn't know what to make of her.

Maybe this came from having a European lover—she was used to loving more cultured than he could provide.

He put a firm hand on her lower back and drew her to him.

Her soft gasp made him hesitate.

Her eyes flew open, and when she swallowed, her throat pulsed at a tiny sliver of vein visible at a fold of her collar.

Was it even possible that she wasn't as sophisticated as she had indicated? But no, he thought, what possible reason would she have for misleading him?

Why would a woman claim to be more sexually experienced than not?

He touched her lips with his. He had never felt such softness before, and a swift primal reaction rose up from his loins.

He kissed her again, this time not for show or for practice or for keeping his job. No, this was for him, because something about her delicate scent or the way her lips yielded to his drove him on. He kissed her, his mouth guiding hers to open, and his tongue touched the gently serrated teeth and then the core softness of her mouth.

And then suddenly he stopped. Withdrew. Kept one hand firmly on her back to steady her, but pulled his head back as far as his own physiology would allow.

"Sorry," he said, his mouth unexpectedly dry and words difficult to manage. "That was more than strictly necessary. It might take a while for me to figure out what's right and what's wrong. When we're strictly colleagues, the line is pretty clearly drawn. But this is a little more murky."

"No, no, that's quite all right," she said, burying her face in his chest. "My fault. I wasn't ready."

"No, if it's anybody's fault, it's mine," he said steadily. "We kissed. I liked it a little too much. That's all. But it was just a kiss. And you know what they say."

She looked up, met his gaze and then laughed.

"A kiss is just a kiss."

"Exactly. And now we're in practice," he said.

"Or at least we won't bump our noses into each other if we need to do it again."

She nodded enthusiastically.

"This is my car," she said, tapping her keys on the hood of a small, blue hatchback. "I should get home. I have to call our man in the Bahamas tomorrow about a new chef and they're four hours ahead of us."

He didn't want to let go of her, but he knew another moment of her in his arms...and he wouldn't be able to stop himself from kissing her again. And again.

She seemed unsteady, but a glance down proved the problem was merely that her right foot had slipped out of its shoe.

"You know, your job is not at issue," he said.

She looked at him with an unreadable expression.

"I know."

"It's mine that's the problem."

"I know that, too."

"If you ever wanted to back out, I'd understand."

"I'm your friend, remember?"

"So we'll go out in the afternoon together. Would that still be okay?"

"Sure," she said, sliding into the driver's seat. "You make the appointment with Gascon."

"Uh, Patricia," he said, hanging on to the door. "Thank you. Again. Thank you."

She nodded. He closed the door. Without another glance at him, she drove away.

Sam stared after her car for a long time after it disappeared down 24th Street.

"Get your car, sir?" A valet approached.

"No, no, that's all right," he said. "I'll find it myself."

What did she want from him? On the way to his home on the outskirts of the city, he kept asking the question. He concentrated so hard, he forgot his exit on the highway and had to double back.

He had always thought of Patricia as a relative innocent, maybe a little spinsterish—although he'd never admit to such a politically incorrect term—and a tad prim for his tastes. Over the past six months he'd certainly developed a certain protectiveness towards her. As if she were the younger sister he never had.

Yes, he thought of her as a sister—affection and lighthearted fun suffusing their relationship.

He had certainly never regarded her as complicated or mysterious.

But now he wondered if under those stiffly starched blouses and dress-for-success suits there lurked a woman of experience, culture and sophistication he could hardly imagine.

And his hard scrabble life had made him leery of asking for favors. What did she want from him? What did she want in return for participating in this crazy charade? Money, a promotion, a job transfer?

Whatever it was, Sam vowed he'd give it to her.

Chapter Six

Patricia opened the copy of *Vogue* and turned to the page she had marked with a folded corner.

"That's what I want. Not the body piercing, but everything else."

Sitting across from her at his gilt consulting table, Gascon sniffed and then shook his head.

"She has no eyebrows," he said. "That might look good on the runway, but not in real life. I've heard she had them removed permanently."

"Yuck! All right, there's another one," Patricia said, flipping to another page. She had picked up the *Vogue* at the convenience store after dinner with Sam and given herself a crash course in chic. "I want to look like her. But not with the black lipstick."

Gascon turned the magazine around and studied

the model. His pencil-thin lips twitched disapprovingly.

"Too severe," he said. "Fine if you want to run a maximum-security prison, but not suitable for...Sam's woman."

"Then, well, what would you suggest?" Patricia asked, sure that her face had turned the same shade of pink as the wallpaper in the salon.

"Do you trust me?"

Patricia studied Gascon. The whippet-thin owner had enthusiastically greeted her in the lobby, escorting her to his office for what he called "face time." From the way other women stared as they walked through the salon, face time was a rare and precious commodity.

"You're Sam's friend," Patricia pleaded. "What does he want a woman to look like?"

"Yes, I am Sam's friend. We grew up very poor, so poor that a man as successful as Sam could be forgiven for forgetting me. But he's not like that—he loaned me the money to open this shop. I will always be grateful."

"Would you make me beautiful...for him?"

Gascon smiled.

"I cannot make you beautiful, Patricia. God has already done his job. I do my job—I give you a little ooomph!"

Ooomph! sounded like something Sam liked in a woman.

Three hours later, Gascon unlocked the door of the salon to let Sam in. Sam had just come from the office and wore khakis, a navy blue polo shirt, and his blazer was slung over his shoulder.

"Hey, man, how's it going?" Sam asked, and the two men embraced. "Sorry I'm late. Is Maria going to be upset?"

"Perhaps. It's mah-jongg night and I'm supposed to take care of the kids."

"Give her my apologies. I'll just take Patricia," Sam said. He did a double take at the long cool drink of blonde who approached from the end of the salon. He pulled off his aviator frames and blinked against the shimmering apparition. "Who's the dame?"

The blonde's do was an elaborate upsweep with tendrils softening her high cheekbones. She wore a desert rose silk dress with a thigh-high slit that revealed and concealed at every step. Sam's mouth fell open. Could this head-turning, earth-quaking, double-wolf-whistle-worth, traffic-stopping woman possibly be...

"Patricia?"

"You don't have to act as if it's such a shock," Gascon advised quietly.

But it was. He had never seen her looking this way. And yet, the first thought that came to him was that this Patricia could have any man she wanted—certainly didn't have to spend her Friday night helping him on his quest to assuage Rex's worries about his personal life.

"Sam? Are you all right?" Patricia asked.

"I'm just blown away."

She smiled, the kind of smile he liked in her, the kind that made her freckles go pop! with color.

"Really?"

"Yeah, really."

"By me?"

"Oh, yes by you."

"By me," she repeated in wonder.

"Enough," Gascon said, breaking up the ensuing silence. "Out of here, you two. My wife will kill me if I make her late for mah-jongg."

"Thank you, Gascon," Patricia said.

"My pleasure," Gascon replied, kissing her hand. "Oh, nice diamond. Glad to see it on your hand instead of on Melissa's. Now remember, no more of that nail biting. You'll ruin my manicurist's hard work and she'll be heartbroken."

"I promise."

"And here," Gascon said, holding up a plastic bag with a faintly disapproving sniff. "Your suit."

Sam grabbed the bag, reaching a hand in to touch the familiar and reassuring gray gabardine and white oxford blouse. He looked out onto the sidewalk, where Patricia walked out to gather more than her fair share of wolf whistles, head-turns and honking car horns. He looked in the bag. Patricia Peel was a dependable, responsible, no-nonsense co-worker who didn't draw much attention to herself even as she got her work done. She was a living embodiment of gray gabardine suits, sensible shoes and high-collared blouses.

At least she was when she was in the office.

And then there was the Patricia Peel who was bringing traffic to a stop on Alejandro Street. The Patricia Peel who was provoking him to stare, open-mouthed and slack-jawed. The Patricia Peel who was making him hard—as a dozen images of her in his bed...

Whoa! Wait one minute there, buster, he thought. He had never in his career had an errant thought about a colleague. He kept his personal life strictly personal. And his work life strictly...work. In fact, the friendship with Patricia was in itself an oddity, but only one that developed because he had been so darned sure that it wouldn't grow into anything more.

But the woman standing on the sidewalk looked...

"Dangerous," Gascon said. "You're playing a very dangerous game."

Gascon was the only friend Sam had confided in concerning his engagement.

"I'm just beginning to realize just how dangerous."

"But it's a beautiful danger," Gascon said. "Now, out of my shop. I face danger of my own kind if I don't get home."

"Bill me for today?"

Gascon shrugged. Sam walked out onto the fiery hot sidewalk.

Sam had gone out with models and actresses, so he was used to a woman who ignored strangers' primitive tributes to beauty. Patricia seemed flustered, even embarrassed—especially when a man in a passing car hung out the driver's-side window and shouted "Baby, I love you!" She seemed utterly inexperienced at getting so much attention—in fact, she looked like she was in agony.

"My car's parked on the next block," he said, taking her arm since she looked as if she might bolt. "Sorry I'm late. I was on the phone with Vail. The stores are closing, so we'll have to buy a gown for the party tomorrow. I thought we'd have some dinner and, if you're up to it, we could go to my house. I have a collection of Pueblo artwork that you should see. Rex helped me select two items from a charity auction last month."

He was just about to tell her more when he noticed a familiar figure at the news kiosk on the next block. Mildred Van Hess with her nose in a copy of *Phoenix Life*. At least it looked like Mildred. The professional suit draped at the kneecap, the subtle bouffant, the trim figure. Had to be her. If he could just steer Patricia around the next corner.... Suddenly, Mildred looked up as if a hunting dog sensing the presence of her master's prey.

No time to run for cover.

"Patricia, I hope you'll forgive me for what I'm about to do."

He grabbed her around her waist, tugged hard to his chest and kissed her. Really kissed her. She startled, twisted her head as if to get away, and he steadied her with his fingers at the back of her head.

Gascon's long afternoon's work was ruined in an instant as cascades of curls tumbled out of their pins. She moaned, and suddenly surrendered to his kiss. Opened her mouth to take his tongue and he found himself kissing for the pleasure of it—barely remembering that he was doing this for the benefit of Rex's trusted assistant. It wasn't until he relinquished her that Patricia remembered she was on a crowded thoroughfare—otherwise, she would have begged for more. She looked up into his eyes and saw warmth mingled with surprise.

Had he come to his senses? Had he spent last night tossing and turning just as she had? Had he figured out that she loved him and had he realized the same for himself?

How else to explain his sudden impulsive kiss?

"Sorry," he said, glancing over her shoulder.

"Oh, no, Sam, I should tell you that I've always felt like…"

She noticed he wasn't listening, that his eyes were gazing far away.

"Good, she's gone."

She felt just like a balloon popping.

"Who's gone?"

"Mildred Van Hess."

"Mildred? What would she be doing around here?"

"I swear I saw her. She was standing at the kiosk."

"But it's just past five—she wouldn't leave the office earlier than six or seven."

"I'm surprised too, but I could have sworn that was her. No, don't look now. She saw us and I kissed you when she looked up. There. She's across Alejandro—and now she's in that shoe store. If it's her."

He let go of her.

Humiliated and confused, Patricia tried to put back together the hairdo Gascon had worked so hard to create.

"Leave it," Sam said. "It looks great either way. Thanks for being a good sport about letting me kiss you. I saw her but didn't have enough time to warn you."

"No problem," Patricia said quietly. She could kick herself. What a fool she was to think that Sam would notice her—even with three hours of manicuring, hairstyling, makeup and new clothes.

Good sport? He called her a good sport?

It would take more—although, with her lack of experience, she had no idea what the "more" was.

The kiss had affected her much more than it had him. She blinked away a tear and squeezed her finger against the corners of each eye so that the thin layer of mascara wouldn't run.

"Ready for dinner?" Sam asked.

"Sure."

"Friends?" He held out his hand.

Maybe this is all I'll ever have with him, Patricia thought. And she knew that as much as she loved Sam, she also liked him. If all he had to offer was friendship, she still could be...

"Friends."

They shook.

No, she thought, she wouldn't give up. That kiss was just the beginning....

Driving to the El Matedor with Sam's BMW's top down disassembled what remained of Gascon's work—but the mark of the stylist's genius was such that when the valet opened the passenger door and Patricia stepped out, a quick toss of her hair created the same effect many women spent hours at the stylist to achieve.

Dinner was suitably delicious—Patricia relaxed as she realized this was little different than the many business dinners and quick take-out meals they had shared together.

Of course, Sam didn't usually have trouble stringing words together to make complete sentences. And Sam didn't usually lose his train of thought and simply say "Wow" at odd intervals.

Of course, he could be tired. Patricia certainly was. It had been an exhausting two days, so when Sam suggested that they go to his home after dessert, she nearly said no. A glance at her watch confirmed that it was after ten.

But Rex's retirement party was the coming evening, and if she was going to talk intelligently about the Pueblo art that Rex had encouraged Sam to buy, she'd better see it now.

The desert air was cool and crisp. The drive was soothing and she took little notice of how her thoughts drifted to nothingness. When he pulled onto the private lane leading to his house, she didn't hide her admiration.

The architecture was Spanish Colonial, pale stucco walls roofed in clay.

"I bought it five years ago," Sam explained. "It hadn't been lived in for nearly twenty years. I fixed it up, starting with the broken clay pipes and evicting the roadrunners and jackrabbits living in the attic. I hired half the folks from my old neighborhood to pull it together."

"It's beautiful," she said. They got out of the car and walked across the cobblestone courtyard to the heavy mesquite door.

"Tell Rex you've always loved the fountain," Sam said, pointing to a cherub spouting water from its mouth into a grassy pond. "He bought me that as a housewarming present."

"I'll remember," Patricia promised.

He unlocked the door and escorted her into a tiled foyer. He flipped the switch to a twelve-armed iron chandelier hanging from the living room ceiling.

"Have a seat," he suggested, throwing his keys onto a Mexican altar table that served as a console. "I'll make us some coffee."

What looked most comfortable—a long, chintz-covered chaise—turned out to be most comfortable. Its plush cushions were stuffed with down. Patricia pulled her dress down as low as it would go and kicked off her heels.

She heard Sam as if from a long distance away—running water, opening and closing a refrigerator, calling to her to inquire if she took cream or sugar. She didn't answer immediately, because it seemed to take a great effort to remember that she didn't even drink coffee.

She thought Sam was talking to her, telling her that he was such an oaf to have kept her up past her bedtime.

His scent seemed so much more vivid than it did when she was...dreaming.

She was going to get her man.

This was the time, this was the week—heck, this was the night.

Chapter Seven

"Sam, I love you," she murmured. "I always have."

He growled, low in his throat.

Desire—satisfied once, twice, three times through the night—moved him to knead the soft compliant flesh of her hips.

He smelled of musk and passion and coffee....

Coffee?

Patricia sniffed the sharp scent of coffee touched by chocolate. She stretched, feeling light-as-air silk sheets caressing her naked legs.

I haven't had such a good night's sleep in... She opened her eyes and sat bolt upright.

Oh, dear, what had she done?

The spacious bedroom she found herself in was bathed in a rose-colored glow—through ivory lace curtains sunlight dappled the sponged walls. The bed was intricately carved teak covered by a Navaho print blanket. In the corner of the room was a mission chest of drawers and a Tiffany-style lamp. A collection of sports trophies and ribbons were displayed on three shelves jutting out of the wall. An ocotillo-branch-shuttered window overlooked the downstairs great room.

Unmistakably this was Sam's bedroom.

What had she done? What had he done?

Her memory of the previous evening was as clear as a bell, up to and including waiting in Sam's chair for a cup of coffee—but she couldn't remember getting into bed.

With him? Without him?

Although the dress Gascon had picked out for her, now hiked up around her hips, had never had enough fabric to make what she would consider a suitable guest towel, the fact that the dress was still on her, zippered up to the top, and her panties were on her hips gave her some measure of comfort.

Even as she came to the contradictorily disappointing conclusion that nothing, nothing at all had happened.

But there was the dream. And though she often dreamt of him, dreams she would never reveal to anyone under the most daunting torture, she was certain that last night's dream was somehow different.

More vivid. More certain.

More real?

If it was real, then he must know.

Know everything.

Everything about her, not just the stuff they could talk about over a dinner table.

Did he think she was a freak? A woman on the shelf past her sell-by date? A dried-up *spinster*—to use an old-fashioned term?

Worse, did he think she was an innocent who couldn't be his match?

I gotta get out of here and do some serious thinking, she decided, standing up and giving her dress a good sharp tug. Shoes. Purse. Keys. Nothing.

She looked under the bed, on top of the chest of drawers, under the blanket she had so forcefully thrown back. She even crawled up under the bed.

"Finding everything you need?" Sam asked.

She whirled and stood, taking care to jerk the hem of her dress over her panties. He lounged at the doorjamb, wearing khakis and a gently faded orange polo shirt. The cup of coffee in his hand looked tempting. It might clear her head.

Her head definitely needed clearing. How could she ask him *if* and *if so, how was it?*

"How do you…feel this morning?" she asked, standing up and taking the coffee.

"Well rested." He beamed. "I hadn't realized how tense I had been all week with this Rex matter. With all that tension relieved, I feel great. How 'bout you?"

Patricia stared.

"Tension relief? Last night was tension relief?"

"Oh, yeah," he agreed happily. "I felt better than I have in weeks."

"So it's just a physical thing."

Sam licked his lower lip.

"Sure. Of course it is. Why would it be anything else?"

"Don't you ever feel any…reverence for it?"

Sam thought long and hard.

"You know, I must. Because I've always thought I have to have a good pillow."

"I gotta go," she snapped, tugging her hair back into a no-nonsense ponytail and then discovering that she didn't have a scrunchie—not even a rubber band. She let her hair fall around her shoulders and decided from his appreciative gaze that she was only making matters worse.

"I thought I knew you, Sam," she said.

"You did. But now we know each other better."

"Is that all that last night was—knowing each other better? And physical tension relief?"

"Great combination, wasn't it?"

"I'm gone."

"I'll drive you back to Gascon's to pick up your car," he said, shrugging amiably. "Want some breakfast first?"

"I think I should go. Now."

She squeezed past him.

"Patricia, are you all right?" he asked, following her downstairs into the living room. "You seem…agitated. Do you want to reconsider this deal? I could call Rex at home right now and explain that Melissa and I broke up and that she won't be coming to the retirement party."

"I'm fine," she insisted.

Sure I'm fine. I've just discovered that the man I've apparently given my virginity to—what an old-fashioned phrase but it's so true!—thinks making love to me is the equivalent of a hearty thirty minutes on the exercise bike or twenty in the whirlpool.

Oh, Patricia Peel, how could you be so foolish? You were always the smart and sensible type.

One shoe was by the couch. She got down on her hands and knees to look for the other.

"I can't remember anything about last night!" she wailed, giving in to frustration.

"What's there to remember?" Sam asked. "We had dinner, we came back here."

"It's the 'came back here' part that I can't remember! The physical tension relief part."

"You mean sleep?"

"Before that."

"There wasn't any before that."

She looked up from her perusal of the underside of his couch. She was about to tell him that there was a quarter under there, as well as a paperback and a pencil. Informing him of the location of household objects would have to wait.

"Nothing happened?"

"Nothing."

"As in really nothing?"

"Absolutely really nothing."

She should feel happy. Pleased. Relieved—physically or mentally or both.

Instead she felt oddly let down.

"Not even an itsy bitsy opposite of nothing?"

"No. You went to sleep."

"I know that part."

"In the chair, right there."

She glared accusingly at the chair as if it were to blame.

"And then what?" she asked, lunging for the shoe that peeked out from under the upholstery.

"And then I thought you'd get a crick in your neck sleeping there, so I carried you to the bed."

"You carried me?" The images that went through Patricia's mind smacked of *Gone with the Wind.* But involved a lot less fabric than Scarlet's dress. "In your arms?"

"Tough to do with my feet."

She stood up, shoving her toes into her shoes and picked up another four inches in height. Still, she had to tilt her head back to meet his gaze. How had Gascon persuaded her to give up her sensible heels for stilettos? Stilettos that were impossible last night and not any easier today.

"And then nothing." He put down the coffee cup on the hutch and steadied her balance. "I went to sleep in the guest room."

"You did? Is that where the tension release comes in?"

"Best night of sleep I've gotten in a week," Sam said. "Patricia, you think I would take advantage of you? Of our friendship?"

Actually, no.

But now she wondered if she should worry that he hadn't.

"I'm sorry," she said, letting her shoulders relax. "I was a little confused. Waking up in a man's house, your house. I'm sorry."

"Try this."

He gave her the coffee and with a strong, sure hand beneath her elbow, guided her through sliding glass doors to the patio that overlooked the desert valley. He offered her a cushioned rattan chaise by the kidney-shaped pool. The water looked cool and soothing.

"I was just finishing up preparing breakfast," he said. "I'll bring it out here. We have another hour before the heat sets in."

Patricia Peel, get a grip on yourself, she thought as he disappeared through the shuttered doors to the kitchen. She sipped her chocolate-laced coffee and breathed in the sun-baked desert air. A whisper-weight wind, scented with the late blooming succulent flowers and cooled by the night, drifted from the mountains.

She was used to dreaming about Sam and then having to put her dreams in a precious little box during the day—she just wasn't used to doing the dreaming in his bed and putting the dreams in a box while he watched!

Sam returned with a tray laden with two plates of fruit, thick toast and eggs scrambled with sausage and hot peppers. Patricia felt composed enough to help out by getting the pitcher of orange juice and two glasses from the kitchen counter.

"To tonight," Sam said, touching his glass to hers. "The retirement party. I can't tell you how grateful I am to you. Whatever I can do for you in return, name it."

"Sam, no, I'm not that mercenary."

"I know that, but is there anything in return you want?"

"Nothing," she said, shaking her head.

"No?"

"Well, okay, something."

"Name it," he said, setting his jaw sternly. "It's yours."

"I want one of your shirts because I don't feel quite dressed this morning. Gascon's idea of hem length is rather indecent."

"Patricia, darling, where have you been?" Her mother's question was the first thing Patricia heard when she picked up the phone. "I've been calling all night."

"Mother, I'm sorry, I just walked in the door."

"It's one o'clock in the afternoon," her mother said, continuing without the slightest trace of maternal pique, "I sure hope you were having fun."

"I was at...at a friend's house."

"Is your friend male?"

"Well, yes, but I slept most of the time."

"Oh, heavens, I wish you'd move to Paris. Frenchmen are not nearly so boring as Americans."

"Mother, it's not like that," Patricia said, flipping through the caller ID screen. Her mother's Paris number showed up twenty-four times.

When Sam had dropped her off at Gascon's parking lot after a quick shopping trip for the perfect party dress, he had kissed her on the cheek.

There wasn't really any need for more practice at romantic kissing.

And the high five that they ordinarily gave each other when saying goodbye seemed not quite enough to acknowledge their conspiratorial closeness.

How could their relationship ever be the same? And yet, how could it be any more intimate when Sam regarded her as a friend—and not even a close enough friend to do him a favor without expecting something in return?

I'm going to have to leave Barrington and Phoenix when this is over, Patricia thought with sudden, heartbreaking clarity. To stay would be too humiliating, too raw.

And to one day watch him make another woman Mrs. Sam Wainwright would be too painful.

Unless, by some miracle, he came to know how deeply she felt and he did a one-eighty on his feelings. Unless she succeeded at showing him that she was the woman for him. She tugged at the sleeve of his shirt, sniffing the slight scent of him. The memory of that scent would live with her long after she returned the shirt.

"Patricia, are you listening?"

"Sorry, Mom. What were you saying?"

"I called last night because I'm thinking of taking a weekend to fly in to see you. I assumed you'd be home by seven o'clock on a Friday night. Even if the rest of the world dates."

"Mom!"

"And then I called back at eight o'clock, and then eight-thirty... You know, Patricia, for all your skills in language and diplomacy and all the traveling you did with me and your father, I'm surprised you're not more adventurous in your social life. But I hope last night means you're catching up."

"What weekend are you thinking of?" Patricia asked, wearily deflecting her mother's lecture.

"Next weekend."

"Sure, I don't have any plans." Patricia gulped. She'd still be officially engaged—Rex wasn't leaving for his world cruise for two weeks. It wouldn't help to have her mother around. "Mom, I forgot. I'm really busy at work."

"What about the weekend after that?"

Patricia did some quick calculations.

"I don't think so. Maybe a little later—toward fall."

"You're more busy with this new friend than you'd like to admit."

"No, Mom, I'm not busy with him."

"That's all right. Say what you want. But I'm a mom and I know what's going on. I'm happy for you. I'll call back in a few days and see if there's a convenient time I can come. Au revoir! And as I hear these teens say, 'Go for it'!''

As Patricia let the phone slip back to the receiver, the garment bag with the retirement-party dress, her briefcase and the previous day's mail fell to the floor.

"I'm not a 'go for it' kind of person," she told her empty apartment.

Oh, yes, you are, a small voice inside her said. What was that word Cindy had used—*hussy?* Maybe just a little. Maybe just for Sam. Now she just needed a little follow-through. After all, she said yes to Sam's proposal, however businesslike he meant it. Not quite as forward-thinking as the sixty percent of women in the *Arizona Republic* poll, but not like the four percent who considered it wrong for women to take the initiative in a relationship.

"I guess I am a 'go for it' person," Patricia said. "At least when it comes to Sam."

And she squared her shoulders, picked up the garment bag and briefcase and went to the bedroom at the back of the apartment.

Turning the radio on to the most provocative music she could find, she figured she had just over six hours to daydream and to turn herself into the most glamorous, beautiful woman Sam had ever seen.

Because there was a spark of something when they kissed—maybe she was the only one who felt it because she was a virgin, more sensitive to these things. But if there was a spark, surely it could be ignited to flame.

And if she failed, and if Sam simply gave her a high five and a "thank you very much" at the end of their engagement, at least she'd know she tried her best to win the heart of the man she loved.

Chapter Eight

Adjusting the cuffs on his white pleated formal shirt, Sam caught himself whistling a romantic Harry Connick, Jr. ballad.

"Sam Wainwright, you're losing your mind," he told the mirror. "This is business. Business. Business. Business."

On the dresser was his list. He had made a list for every Barrington party he had ever attended. Even after fifteen years he didn't trust himself to remember all the people who needed a pat on the back and the new hires he needed to make introductions for.

He reviewed tonight's list:

1. Compliment the VP from Texas on getting the Dallas Barrington Spa up and running two months ahead of schedule.

2. Congratulate Lucas Hunter in the legal department and his wife, Olivia, on their pregnancy.

3. Bring together Kyle Prentice from the New Product Division with the manager of the Key West facility—Key West is looking for some help from NPD.

4. Congratulate Sophia Shepherd on her new position as Rex III's assistant (has she seen him?). Formally introduce her to Mike from the mail room.

Sam puzzled over entry number four. Then he remembered that the young man who delivered the mail to his office twice a day had specifically mentioned that he thought Sophia was a dish but that she seemed hesitant about talking to him.

Sam usually limited his party list to things that would help the corporation—playing matchmaker wasn't on his job description. But Mike seemed awfully nice and Sam couldn't help wanting to lend a hand.

"Why am I doing this?" he asked aloud. "Have I turned into Cupid?"

He was supposed to be thinking corporate. In fact, the little reminders that he set up for the party paled compared to the most important corporate task he had set before him this evening: introduce Patricia to Rex as his fiancée.

This goal was so important, so vital to his future that he crumpled up his list and threw it away. His job was everything to him, more than the paycheck or even the prestige or the satisfaction he got from being the best at what he did.

No, his job was an affirmation that he wasn't just a dirt-poor barrio boy. He had overcome every obstacle—poverty, a public school that didn't have enough money to buy books, the temptation of gangs that recruited from his playmates, the long hours working two part-time jobs to get through college.

He fingered the framed letter on the wall over his dresser. It was sixteen years old, smudged on the letterhead, creased twice so that it would have fit into a business-size envelope. But it was more precious to him than any masterpiece.

It was his letter from Rex II welcoming him to the Barrington family. "You have a fire inside you, the kind that makes a man do great things. You're going to make me proud, Sam, as proud as I am of my own son who is just your age but has never been tested by circumstances the way you have. I would be honored if you would take a position in our company—if you do, I assure you that the sky is the only limit to your ambition and hard work."

When Sam had received that letter, he had shouted so loudly that his neighbors had dialed 911—the neighborhood was not unfamiliar with violence. He had had to explain to the police and to the crowd that gathered outside his one-room apartment that he had gotten his dream job.

Everything Sam did he did to make Rex proud of

his decision to hire him. Sam was first in the office in the morning and the last to leave at night. He went to Rex's tailor with his first paycheck and to Rex's custom shirt store with his second. Sam cultivated a taste in wines, Navaho art and Colonial Spanish interiors—just like Rex II.

In fact, Rex was the reason he had found Melissa Stanhope so attractive—she was from a good family, was beautiful and very cultivated. And yet Rex II was also why Sam had broken up with Melissa— Rex II felt his wife, dead now for fifteen years, had been his soul mate. Sam knew that he and Melissa were so different that he could never even grow to describe her that way. She wasn't a soul mate, she was a trophy.

What would Rex think of Patricia as a fiancée? Sam wondered as he pulled on his black tuxedo jacket and patted down the sleek lapels.

She was beautiful, friendly, hardworking, utterly without a mean bone in her body. What a contrast to Melissa. In fact, Sam thought as he walked downstairs, Rex II would say that Patricia was made for him.

Sam paused at the Mexican altar table in the center hall. He had been looking for his keys but now keys didn't seem so important.

Patricia made for him?

This charade had gone too far.

"We're not talking about a real fiancée," Sam said.

He swiped his keys from the table, flipped on the

security system and headed out into the blazing heat. As he got into his car, he wondered if this deception was a terrible idea.

He could, he should, he would tell Rex that he had broken up with Melissa. That he had no fiancée, no girlfriend, no prospects of marriage.

But the focus tonight should be on Rex, not on Sam's marital status. And if Patricia on his arm made Rex happy and convinced that Sam was still a good hire, then so be it.

Sam drove down Lonesome Trail Drive to pick up Patricia. As he approached her apartment building, he felt unaccountably happy. He even bought flowers from a vendor who walked between cars at the intersection of Missouri and 23rd Street.

Sam handed her the flowers first thing when he entered her apartment.

"Here," he said gruffly. "Don't know why I got them. Put them in water."

Patricia suppressed a smile.

"Are they for me?"

Sam shrugged.

"It's an advance thank-you for all you're doing tonight."

Patricia took the flowers to the kitchen and put them in a vase. Flowers were flowers. It was a start.

She came back out into the living room. As unadventurous as she was in her social life, Patricia had a taste for the exotic in her furnishings.

A leather-and-teak Zulu bed from Africa dominated the room, but it was complemented nicely by a gilded bamboo temple throne from Bangkok and a woven rattan chaise from Egypt.

These starkly elegant pieces were softened with huge pillows and neck rolls made from white matellase fabric Patricia had shipped from a tiny shop in Switzerland near the boarding school where she had spent her middle school years.

"Remember? My parents were diplomats," she said, putting the flowers on a table in front of the window. "So my apartment looks a little like the United Nations."

"It's very nice," Sam said, and then he gave her the once-over, twice, as she twirled in front of him. "You look great, Patricia. You're going to be the belle of the ball."

For the retirement party, Patricia had chosen a more conservative dress than she had worn the evening before. Her dress was a pale green chiffon that hugged her breasts and draped in a handkerchief hem at her ankles. Gascon had taught her how to make a French twist and although strands fell around her pale bare neck, she had managed to corral most of her thick mane. She had followed Gascon's makeup suggestions to a T—even wearing an icy pink lipstick that made her lips look full and pouty.

"Wow," Sam said simply.

Patricia had never liked having a small apartment, but housing prices being what they were in Phoenix, this cramped one-bedroom was all she could afford.

But for the first time in six months, Patricia blessed skyrocketing rents, profit-oriented landlords and even the international clutter that she had accumulated in twenty-nine years as a diplomat's daughter.

When Sam stood up, he was close. So close that her breasts just grazed the pleats of his crisp, white shirt. Only a thin pale line of gray surrounded the deep dark circle of his eyes. He held his hands out at either side as if almost, almost ready to embrace her.

She took a chance, a big one, and kissed him lightly on the lips.

"For practice," she said huskily, with every smidgen of sophistication she could muster.

He didn't say a word, didn't shy away, didn't even remind her that they had already done some practicing.

Instead, he swept her into his arms and kissed her. Really kissed her. As if to show her how it was really done.

And he did.

Her willing mouth surrendered to his lips, to his tongue, to his teasing of senses that she hadn't even known she possessed. His hardness was pressed against her abdomen and if this was practice, the main event both frightened and excited her.

When he relinquished her, it was several seconds before either one of them recovered enough to speak.

"I'm sorry..." he started to say, but she put a

finger to his lips. Those beautiful, strong lips that were still wet with her color and her touch. "For practice," he said at last.

"For practice," she agreed.

They both knew that if they left her apartment now they'd arrive at the party on time and not fashionably fifteen minutes late. Still, when Sam offered her her tiny white beaded evening bag, she didn't say a word.

Instead, she thought with emerging joy—there was something there, something in our kiss. He feels something. Something that might become love if I can just be the woman he wants me to be.

Although Barrington Corporation events were generally held in Barrington quarters, the Phoenix Barrington was a small, intimate spa and utterly too cozy for a party as large and as lavish as Rex's retirement, one that included every employee, from the high-powered vice presidents to the busboys at the Barrington restaurants. Luckily, the manager of the Phoenician had gotten his start in the resort industry at Barrington Corporation and had closed his hotel's finest restaurant, Mary Elaine's, so that it could be used for the evening.

After dropping off the car with the valet, Patricia and Sam hurried over the bridge of the Necklace Lake, pausing only to admire the honest-to-goodness pearl tiles of the Mother-of-Pearl Pool. They said hello to several people from the accounting department who had gathered early for a drink at the Thirsty Camel Lounge. Sam looked slightly baffled when Rachel, an accountant for the department, offered a toast to his engagement.

"He works so hard, he forgets his personal life sometimes," Patricia said, slipping her arm into the bend of his elbow.

Several people laughed, a few nodded sagely.

"Honey, I have to watch myself," Sam said with mock solemnity. "Some people will think you're not joking."

After remembering to congratulate Rachel and Nick Delaney on their recent wedding, Sam told Patricia they should get to the party.

The restaurant was twinkling with gold candles and beautiful white orchids. The panoramic view of the valley was beautiful this evening. Mildred Van Hess stood at the door with Rex—she looking especially radiant in a beige silk pant suit.

"Well, Sam, my man, it's good to see you," Rex II said, holding out his hand for a high five. "And this... But this is Patricia, your right-hand man— well, woman—in Personnel. It's always wonderful to see a beautiful woman, but I was hoping to meet your fiancée tonight."

Patricia looked up at Sam. He hesitated. Would he 'fess up?

"You are meeting her," he said at last, putting his arm around Patricia's waist. "Rex, may I introduce the future Mrs. Sam Wainwright."

Patricia held out her carefully manicured hand to Rex II. The older man's eyebrows knitted together and Patricia suddenly remembered the encounter outside Sam's office. Did Rex remember?

"I never knew," he said. "I never saw you two together—except, of course, in professional circumstances."

"We were trying to be discreet," Sam said. "These days, it's particularly important for Personnel directors to set a good example."

"Well, you were discreet. So much so I never suspected. Did you, Mildred?"

"I saw them together," Mildred said. "On Alejandro Street."

"Did you really?" Sam asked with utmost casualness.

She nodded fiercely.

Sam wondered if she guessed the truth. She was always very smart, seemed to soak up knowledge about the company, its people and its place in the world. But she never knew about his engagement to Melissa. He was sure of that....

"Mildred, she's perfect for him," Rex said, fairly bubbling. "She's a real beauty, isn't she? And nice, too. You can tell they go together like...like, what's that famous song I'm thinking of?"

Noticing that Rex hadn't let go of Patricia's right hand, Mildred took the younger woman's left hand in her own. She glanced at the diamond. "Like love and marriage."

"That's right!" Rex exclaimed. "That's the song. Love and marriage, marriage and love, go together like a hand and glove..." he sang, elbowing Sam in the ribs.

Sam smiled tightly. Rubbing his palms together, Rex asked, "So when's the big date?"

Chapter Nine

"Big date?" Sam asked, perplexed.

"Your wedding," Mildred prompted archly.

Sam looked at Patricia. She ducked her head. They were going to get caught....

"The sooner the better," he said just as Patricia jerked her chin up and announced, "We haven't set a date yet."

"Hope you agree on other things," Mildred said, snagging a champagne glass from the tray of a passing waiter.

"You lovebirds have to decide soon," Rex counseled. "Can't let love slip out of your fingers. Love and marriage, wish I could remember that song, go together like...what was it again?"

"Hand and glove," Mildred said. She craned her neck to look over Sam's shoulder. "Rex, you're so excited about this party and it's just getting started.

Look at all the people who've come to celebrate with you. Why don't we talk to the couple later about their wedding plans?''

Patricia bobbed her head in agreement.

"Yes, Rex, we shouldn't monopolize your time," Sam said, glancing back at the line of guests who were waiting to enter Mary Elaine's doors. "We'll let you go."

"I'm so happy for you, young man," Rex said, pumping his arm.

"And I'm happy for you, Rex."

With a hand under Patricia's elbow, he guided her to the bar. The bartender asked what they were drinking.

"I'll have a soda, please," Patricia said. She leaned close to Sam and whispered, "I don't want to get tripped up here. This is harder than I thought. Early wedding, late wedding. Why didn't we think about what to say when he asked about weddings?"

"Two sodas," Sam told the bartender. "Because we never thought it would go any further than just an introduction."

"He knows the truth," Patricia said miserably.

"He does not," Sam said. "Although Mildred looks a little suspicious. Please, Patricia, don't worry. I don't think that was too bad. And we probably won't run into them again this evening. Rex is going to be so busy, he won't remember anything except that I have the most beautiful, charming fiancée in the world. Now let's mingle. There's a few people we should say hi to."

Patricia would have followed him anywhere at that point. Beautiful. Charming. Beautiful. Charming. He was noticing her.

They exchanged greetings with several other couples. Sam had kind words for everyone, accepted thanks from several department heads for his help and guidance, and complimented others for work well done. Patricia glowed when so many people told them that they were a perfect couple.

Not just a few confided that they had always suspected a romance—because of the way they got along so well and spent so much time together.

"I'm a lucky man," Sam said in reply to the many congratulations on his engagement. He said it so often that Patricia wondered if he, like she, lost track of the fact that this wasn't a real engagement, that this wasn't a real romance and that their relationship wasn't going any further than it would this night.

As the room grew more crowded, a manager from Dallas asked if Sam would give him some advice on a "sensitive matter." Although Sam encouraged Patricia to stay, and reminded the manager that she was the assistant personnel director for the company, Patricia still read the manager's reluctance even as he apologized for seeming rude.

It was okay with Patricia—there were plenty of women in the company who confided problems to her that they wouldn't dream of talking about in front of Sam. When she said that she really must use the ladies' room, the manager could barely contain his relief.

In the ladies' room, she found her friends from the lunchroom.

"You look so radiant!" Olivia cried out. Clearly uncomfortable at the end of her pregnancy, she sat on a chaise and held out her arms for a hug. "I can't believe you're engaged!"

"Yeah, it's just like a fairy tale," Rachel said, turning from the mirror where she was touching up her lipstick. "I'm so happy for you."

"We've all been living a fairy tale," Cindy said. "I've got my boss, Kyle. Olivia's married to Lucas."

"He wasn't who she thought she was in love with," Molly pointed out. "Remember Stanley Whitcomb? Olivia was certain that he was the man of her dreams."

"I still think he's a nice man," Olivia insisted. "And Lucas gets along with him very well."

"Still, Molly." Rachel hushed her friend. "You've ended up with Jack, who was your boss. Even if you had to get hit on the head doing it."

Molly had been injured in a fight at the advertising department party and had woken up convinced she was Jack's wife. When the dust settled, Jack realized that she was the perfect woman for him.

"And I've married Nick," Rachel continued. "So with Patricia engaged to Sam, there's only one of us still on the marriage market."

All eyes landed on Sophia who was at the mirror, trying her best to tame her curly blond hair.

"Hey, Patricia, is the Third going to make a surprise appearance at the party?" she asked.

"I don't think so," Patricia said. "He's scheduled to be in France today."

Trying not to look too disappointed, Sophia put her lipstick away.

"I'm going to be his bride, you know," she said. "Or, at least, I want to. Do you think he'll notice me?"

"It'd be hard not to if you're his assistant," Patricia said.

"What about Mike the mailman?" Olivia teased.

"Look, I might lust after him," Sophia said. "But lust isn't enough for me."

"The Third could be a jerk," Rachel warned.

"I'm sure he's not," Sophia said. "Just from the memos I've gotten from him, I know he's a nice, sweet, sensitive..."

"Okay, okay." Olivia made peace. "Sophia's right. She should get a chance to marry her boss if that's what she wants to do. By the way, did you see how Mike was talking with Rex? They seemed awfully chummy."

"What would Rex have to say to the mail room guy?" Rachel asked.

"I wonder what his story is—maybe there's a real mystery," Cindy speculated. "Nobody really knows anything about Mike. He's strong and has a commanding presence. Doesn't look like he should be in the mail room. Looks like he belongs in the executive suite. But where'd he come from? What kind of job did he have before he started here? And where'd he get those muscles?"

"Come on, 'fess up," Sophia said, putting an arm around Patricia. "At least tell me about Mike if you can't tell me anything more about the Third."

"I don't know anything," Patricia said, feeling bad that she couldn't help more. "Mike was Sam's personal hire."

"Let me get this straight," Sophia said, disbelief etched in her face. "The vice president of personnel for the whole company, national and international departments included, hires the mail room guy on his own?"

Patricia nodded.

"That sounds weird," Olivia said. "Sam's too important to be dealing with the mail room."

"But he takes a real interest in his people," Patricia said, and then she quieted. "You're right. Vice presidents don't hire the mail room help."

"Ask him Mike's story," Sophia said.

"Mike's personnel files would be confidential, and as the assistant personnel director, I have to respect that confidentiality."

"But you're Sam's fiancée," Sophia pointed out. "That's got to count for something."

"Right, you're his fiancée," Rachel said.

"You guys look great together," Olivia said, her tone making clear that the subject of Mike the mailman was closed. "And it was all so sudden. You just had to tell him how you felt, and the magical thing was that he felt the same way.''

''Yeah,'' Rachel chimed in. ''Just this last weekend, you were so sad, thinking that you'd never get the courage to ask him out. Tell us how it happened again.''

In the corner, Sophia pleaded silently and Patricia nodded.

She'd see what she could do about finding out more about Mike—even as she knew that Sophia would appreciate information about the Third more.

''Patricia, are you listening to us?'' Olivia asked.

''What? Oh, yeah, you were asking how it happened?''

''Yes, start to finish.''

''But it's so boring.''

Rachel put her hands on her hip.

''You call seducing Sam Wainwright in his office and getting an engagement ring on your finger, all before lunch, boring?'' she demanded.

''When you went into his office and when he asked you to marry him,'' Olivia said. ''We want to hear the whole story again. With the details. Just not the X-rated ones.''

''There aren't any X-rated ones.''

The door opened and Mildred Van Hess came in.

''Good evening, girls,'' she said. ''You can't have the whole party in the ladies' room. It's unfair to the men. Although I have to admit that I've appreciated all the attention that's come my way.''

Everyone laughed.

"We were just talking about Patricia and Sam and their whirlwind courtship," Olivia said. "It was all so sudden. You know, last weekend at my baby shower..."

Patricia stared, panic rising in her throat. She would be caught if Mildred Van Hess found out that the "engagement" was thought by her friends to be this week's news, while Rex thought she had been Sam's girlfriend for a while!

"We've all heard enough about these two love-birds." Mildred shushed Olivia. "I want to know how your pregnancy is going."

Olivia was delighted to give Mildred every little detail and when all the women left the ladies' lounge, Patricia was so caught up in the details of Olivia's life that she had nearly forgotten that her own was such a web of deception.

"Would you take a look at Rex and Sam?" Mildred asked, putting her arm through Patricia's. "Sam has always been Rex's favorite hire. And he's so happy that Sam has found the stability of marriage. You're so good for him. He deserves every happiness that life has to offer. I don't know you too well, but I'd suspect the same is true about you."

Patricia had never heard Mildred Van Hess make such a personal evaluation about anyone, and it got her to thinking about the valued assistant to the boss.

"Mildred, what are you going to be doing when Rex retires?"

"I got a great pension," Mildred said. "I suppose

I'll take up a hobby. Gardening, maybe. Or postage stamps. Or ballroom dancing.''

She briskly guided Patricia to the two men, who appeared to have been in the middle of an intense conversation. Patricia felt her heart begin to gallop. Sam had thought that the conversation at the beginning of the party would be their only contact with Rex. But now…

"Ah, Patricia, glad you're back," Sam said, an oddly strained look on his face that was at odds with his easy words. "Rex has just made us the most astoundingly generous offer."

"Really?" Patricia asked, trying to look casual as Sam kissed her cheek and whispered, "it's okay, we'll get through this."

"Oh, I hope you don't mind an old man's meddling," Rex said. "But I was telling Sam here that I don't want to miss your wedding because I'm on my world tour. Likewise, I don't want to have to miss the Great Wall of China or the pyramids at Cheops to watch you two tie the knot when you can do it right now."

"Right now?" Patricia said, squelching the pure terror that she was experiencing.

"Well, not this very moment," Rex clarified. "Although it's tempting, isn't it? I'm talking about sometime in the next two weeks. Before I leave. Do it at my home. It would give me the greatest pleasure you can imagine. And then I will take my cruise knowing that my company and my employees and my friend Sam are in the best hands."

Sam looked at Patricia helplessly.

"We can't," Patricia said softly. "Uh, Sam's always wanted a very…large wedding. And those take so much planning."

"Actually, he said it was you that wanted the big wedding but that he'll go either way." Rex chuckled. "Just so long as it's legal."

"Then there's another problem." Sam scrambled for an excuse. "Her mom is in the diplomatic corps. Very remote part of the world. Jungles and mountainous terrain. Can't get a flight out in two weeks. Where is she again, darling?"

"France."

"They do have transportation difficulties," Mildred said dryly.

Sam hung his head.

"Okay, I should confess to you the truth. Rex, I love you dearly," Sam said. "You gave me a chance when no one else would. I owe my life to you. I'd never have made it out of the barrio without your help."

"Oh, Sam, you have so much ambition, sometimes I feel Barrington Corporation's held you back from even greater things."

"No, Rex, I'm happy here. Very happy. Perhaps you won't be so happy with me when I tell you the truth."

The pain in his face moved Patricia, so much so that she swallowed all her qualms and put her fingers to his lips.

"What Sam's saying is that we'd honestly be

so...grateful and honored if you would host our wedding. But we didn't want you to feel obligated."

"Obligated? I'd be honored!"

"You would?" Sam asked.

"Yes, I would!" Rex beamed. "So you'll let me throw you a wedding?"

Patricia looked up at Sam. She nodded encouragingly. The gratitude in his face was so great that Patricia knew it would be worth it.

Even if he never learned to love her, it would be worth it to do this one thing for the man she loved.

He swallowed hard, his Adam's apple throbbing.

"We'd be thrilled," Sam said to Rex. And he squeezed Patricia's hand. "Doesn't a wedding at his home sound great, darling?"

"It sure does," Patricia said.

"I'll help with setting it up," Mildred said. "It'll be fun. Rex, what a way to set off to see the world— a wedding and a bon voyage party all rolled into one!"

Chapter Ten

"Why'd you do it?"

Patricia waved at Rex and Mildred standing on the high-ceilinged portico of the Phoenician's western entrance. Rex had his arm around Mildred and she had dropped her head to his shoulder.

"Do what?" Patricia asked.

"Say you'd marry me at Rex's house."

"I did it because I didn't want to see a grown man cry."

Sam chuckled and guided his car onto the street.

"I wasn't going to cry," he said. "But I was sweating."

"You were going to tell him the truth," Patricia observed. "You were going to tell him that this was a made-up engagement."

"Yeah, I was. I figured it was the right thing to

do when he asked to have the wedding at his home—maybe the only thing.''

"The only other thing is to wait and see,'' Patricia said. ''Maybe he had too much to drink.''

Sam glanced at her.

"No,'' they both said. Rex wasn't much of a drinker.

"Maybe he'll forget about it,'' Sam said.

Patricia glanced at him.

"No,'' they both said. Rex was a follow-through kind of guy. How else could he have started with nothing and created the Barrington corporate empire?

"Maybe he'll get distracted by all the last-minute preparations for his trip,'' Patricia suggested.

"Right. And maybe he'll be abducted by aliens,'' Sam said. ''So why'd you do it? You want Tahiti, right?''

Patricia did a double take.

"Tahiti?''

"Yeah, every person I've ever worked with at Barrington has asked for managing the Tahiti facility. It's yours, Patricia, if you want it. Beaches, clear ocean water, mimosas by the...''

"I'd get a sunburn. See these freckles? They'd turn fuchsia.''

"Switzerland's everybody's second choice.''

"I've been there. Done that.''

"Okay, you want more money.''

"I don't need money,'' Patricia said, starting to get irritated.

"We all need money. Count on getting the max on your bonus—but you would get that anyway because you do good work."

Patricia fumed. She wasn't doing this for a payback. And yet he seemed determined to reduce their relationship to favors given and received.

Tell him, she thought, tell him exactly why you're doing this. You're doing this so he'll take a longer look. So that he'll see you as the woman he deserves, needs...

"I know," Sam said triumphantly, slapping his hands on the steering wheel. "It's my job. You want my job. Well, sister, you can't have it...until I get promoted. And then I'll be happy to move your desk into my office myself."

"That's not it at all."

"Then there's only one other possibility and it makes me very sad. You want to leave."

"Leave?"

"You want to leave and you want a good reference. Patricia, I don't want you to go—I think we work well together, and you're a great friend and I'd miss you. And you're the only woman I know who would agree to go to a fake wedding at Rex's house and know that I couldn't be..."

"Couldn't be what?"

Sam parked the car in her lot.

"Patricia, have you ever thought you might not be the kind of person who could marry?"

Actually, she had been giving that question a lot of thought. Until she met Sam she had assumed that

she could be a good wife…to the right man. And
the right man was simply running late on making
his appearance.

When she fell for Sam, and fell hard, she slowly
realized that she couldn't be a good wife—to any
other man. And if Sam didn't love her, she was
doomed to the single life, because it was unfair to
marry when she'd always measure another man by
Sam's standard.

"I guess I've worried about it," she answered
cautiously. "Is it something you've thought about
yourself?"

"Yes, it is. I've thought about it a lot lately and
I know I can't marry," he said. "Not for real, anyway. That's what I learned from Melissa."

"Not all woman are like Melissa."

"All women need to be loved. I can't love a
woman. Oh, I can go through the motions—and I
did with Melissa. I was attentive, remembered birth-
days and major holidays, was faithful out of habit,
but something was always missing. Me. I was missing."

"Sam, you're too hard on yourself. You won't be
missing…when you're with the right woman. It'll
happen. You're a good man and you'll have it."

"Patricia, you're a real good friend," he said.
"You're the only friend I've got that I can talk about
this kind of stuff with."

He held out his hand and she touched the fingers
in a melancholy facsimile of a high five.

"It's two weeks before Rex leaves," Sam said.

"I can't imagine that this wedding stuff can't be put off. But thank you for agreeing to it. And remember, whatever you want—it's yours. You really are the greatest friend."

She got out of the car and waved as he made a three-point turn out of the drive.

Friend.

The word burned on her thoughts like a branding iron.

Friend.

Now she knew what guys felt like when a woman said, "Let's just be friends." It cut things off, it set a boundary, it put a line in the sand and said this far, no farther.

Friend.

Just friends.

She walked up to her apartment, made herself a cup of cocoa and allowed herself some feeling blue time before she picked herself up for another try.

"Mildred Van Hess is coming over in twenty minutes with some wedding books. What do I tell her?"

Sam opened his eyes and stared at the phone receiver he'd just picked up. It was morning, bright and hot.

"Sam, are you there?"

He stumbled upright, ran his fingers through his hair as if that might jolt him awake and then asked her to repeat herself.

"Mildred Van Hess just called and said she had

some wedding books she wanted me to look at,'' Patricia said, her anxiety fairly crackling the wires. ''She's coming in twenty minutes.''

''To your apartment?''

''Yeah. She said she'd bring a dozen doughnuts, too. Do you want me to tell her that there's no wedding?''

''I guess we have to.''

''She said she's very pleased that the vice president of personnel is marrying, because it's important for Barrington to have a steady guy at the helm, one that embodies our corporate 'families first' spirit.''

''She said all that?''

''On the car phone.''

''Why didn't you tell her you were busy?''

''She said her phone was busted, and she couldn't hear me. Sam, I'm okay with playing along with the wedding thing. I really am. But I don't know what to do when she gets here.''

''You're really okay with it?''

''I told you last night I was.''

''Okay, Patricia, where's your dress?''

''What dress?''

''The one you wore last night.''

''It's in the bag I take to the dry cleaners.''

''Get it out. Oh, and Patricia?''

''Yeah.''

''Put some lipstick on. The same shade you wore last night.''

He hung up, took two steps in one direction, reconsidered, went in the other direction and then took a deep breath.

"This is no time to panic," he said. "This is an opportunity. All calamities are opportunities."

This opportunity still wasn't looking like anything but a calamity—he guessed, in a moment of insight that punctuated his foggy-brained awakening, that Mildred was testing them. If they failed, she'd be sitting at Rex's office tomorrow morning with the news that Sam was not vice president material.

And he'd be at the unemployment office.

He wasted three or four minutes at his dresser, tearing apart his housekeeper's neatly folded system, searching for pajama bottoms before he realized that it had been so long since he wore pajamas that he didn't own any. He settled for cashmere cotton boxer briefs and a pair of low-riding faded jeans.

He threw his own dry cleaner bag onto the floor and yanked out his tux, white dress shirt and located his dress shoes in the kitchen. He tossed all these onto the passenger seat of his car and then remembered the cuff links. And he snagged a toothbrush while he was on his way out for the second time.

All in all, it took nine minutes to get out of the house.

Driving on Lonesome Trail Drive, he stopped repeating his new mantra about calamities being opportunities so that he could brush his teeth, spitting the toothpaste out when he got to the stoplight on Alejandro Street. He had a brief moment of panic when he noticed the shadow on his jawline.

"No, it's the perfect touch," he told himself.

Tires squealing, he ended up at Patricia's apartment house in an Olympic-caliber six minutes. He took the stairs three at a time and pounded on her door.

"You're not wearing a shirt," Patricia said, giving him a long, startled look. "Mildred's coming in a few minutes. You can't be here without a shirt."

"Have you got that lipstick on?"

"Yeah."

"Kiss it," he ordered, holding out his dress white shirt.

"Kiss what?"

"Kiss it!"

He pointed.

"Don't think, Patricia. We don't have time for thinking. Just kiss it."

She tentatively kissed the collar of his shirt. He smudged it a little.

"Good work," he said. "Now where're your shoes?"

"In my closet."

"Get them."

He dropped one of his shoes, by the door, paced out ten steps and threw down another. She returned with a pair of black pumps which he tossed down the hall.

"Aren't you going to put on that shirt?" she asked. She followed him to the kitchen. He reached into his jeans pocket and threw down cuff links and change on the counter.

"What's the matter, you don't like my body?"

He absently looked up from disentangling his dress clothes. He noticed her five-alarm blush. The way her eyes skittered away and then were drawn back to his proud naked chest. For the first time that morning he relaxed, rearing back to give her a good, long look.

"Why, Patricia Peel, I never would have thought this about you, but you're attracted to me."

She pursed her lips. He rested his elbows on the counter and grinned as she held up her evening gown, querying without words what he wanted her to do with it, and then as she let the gown drop to her side.

"It's okay, Tricia. I think you're awfully dandy yourself."

He had her stumped. For the first time since Patricia Peel had come to Barrington, he had her shut up and without any back talk. He could spend hours marveling over this moment. A moment of realization that the straitlaced, dressed-for-success, no-nonsense Patricia Peel had a weak spot for a bare-chested man.

But forget hours—he didn't have a minute for introspection. The doorbell rang, with just that prim, proper trill that meant Mildred Van Hess was on the other side of the door.

Sam shoved his tuxedo jacket and dress pants into his assistant's arms.

"Put this on the floor in your bedroom," he ordered. "With your dress. Is your bed made?"

"Yes, I always…"

"Figures. Unmake it."

In any other instance, Patricia would have asked questions—but she did what she was told. By the time she came back from the bedroom, the doorbell had rung two more ladylike times, and he was lounging on the couch with a cup of coffee and the sports section of the *Arizona Republic*. He tousled his hair for good measure.

"Go ahead and answer it."

"But you don't have a shirt on."

"Answer the door."

She brought her lips together in a particularly prim manner and did as he told her.

"Why, Mildred," he said, flipping down the paper after the women had exchanged greetings. He stood up, rubbed the stubble on his jaw and stretched. "It's so good to see you. Patricia said you two were going to plan the wedding this morning."

Mildred, wearing a pastel suit, stood in the tiny foyer and stared.

"I wasn't expecting you here," she said simply.

He looked down at his bare chest as if noticing for the very first time that he didn't have a shirt on.

"My manners are terrible this morning," he apologized. He picked his dress shirt off the armrest of the bamboo throne. "Do you want a cup of coffee, Mildred?"

Mildred opened her mouth. Closed it. Opened it again. Looked over at Patricia, who gave a perfectly pitched men - can't - live - with - them - can't - live - without - them shrug.

And then Mildred's impeccable manners kicked in.

"Yes, a cup of coffee would be wonderful," she said, and she held up a white bakery box. "I brought some pastries."

"That's great," Sam said, taking the box. "Patricia never keeps good breakfast stuff here."

"How would you—" Patricia started with outrage and ended with a beatific sigh "—like to get Mildred the cup of coffee? Remember, honey, the cups are in the cupboard over the dishwasher."

"I know, darling, I know," he called from the kitchen. "Why don't you take Mildred on a tour of the apartment?"

"But I can't take her in the bedroom," Patricia protested.

He stuck his head back into the foyer and gave the two women what he hoped was a winning smile.

"It's okay, baby. Mildred will understand that we haven't made the bed yet this morning."

Chapter Eleven

Three hours later, with a cheery goodbye and the brisk clip-clop of her sensible heels, Mildred Van Hess left Patricia's apartment.

"That woman could have planned D day," Sam marveled, standing in the doorway with his arm casually draped around Patricia's waist. "I guess that's what makes her such a good assistant for Rex."

"Amazing," Patricia agreed.

"I just have one question," Sam said. "What happens if all those butterflies die?"

"They're overnight expressed in some special packaging," Patricia said. "And Mildred explained that they are released just as you and I get into the limousine to take us to our honeymoon, and it's only twenty-four hours from caterpillar to Arizona sky."

"That's what's supposed to happen. But what if they're dead in the box?"

"I think they can't die because they're hermetically sealed."

"Whatever that means."

"I can't believe she got a list of butterflies native to Arizona so that we'd be helping the ecosystem."

Patricia eased out of his embrace and closed the door.

"So we're really getting married," he said. "Patricia, this has gone too far. I had better confess before Mildred orders those butterflies. Or the cake. Or the dress. Or the caterer."

"Don't. We've gone this far and there's no reason not to go further," she said, picking up Mildred's coffee cup from the table. "We're both sophisticated people. We know how to handle the situation. We'll live together at your place—it's bigger—and get a quiet divorce after a suitable interval."

"Quiet divorce? That sounds stone cold."

"The alternative would be to be together forever."

Sam looked up at her. They were both silent, thinking that forever was a very long time. From the outside, they both looked dubious. Inside, both were more ambivalent.

"I'm really grateful," Sam said. "If it ended now, I know you've done your best."

"I know."

"Anything you want."

"I don't."

"What are you doing?" he asked, coming up behind her just as she bent over to pick up one of his dress shoes. His hands splayed across her hips. She bolted upright and whirled.

"I'm picking up your stuff so you can go," she said. "I'm sure you have a million better things to do than..."

"Oh, no, I'm doing fine right here," he said, and when he stepped forward, she backed up reflexively against her own bedroom door. "We've done a lot of cuddling and kissing and cooing for Mildred's benefit this morning."

It was true. Starting with a kiss when he returned from the kitchen with Mildred's coffee and the platter of pastries. Another to get the raspberry filling he claimed was on Patricia's lips. Hand-holding as they looked at the catalogue of wedding dresses that could be shipped from Paris. He nuzzled her neck while Mildred detailed a dinner menu.

Chicken or fish?

He didn't care, he declared, as he entwined his fingers in Patricia's.

Patricia had been as flustered as, well, a blushing bride-to-be should be.

But the hours had taken their toll and she now felt her control was slipping.

Obviously his was, too.

"So you feel it, too?" she wondered. That he should feel as tingling and achingly ready as she was—it was a marvel. But did it mean, as it did for her, love?

Or was he feeling something more raw and animal-like?

Suddenly she realized she didn't know what to do when male-female relations went beyond a kiss, went beyond a cuddle. That she would be naked before him, powerless before his touch, chained by years of propriety only to have him unleash a mysterious force within her, was too close, too real, too frightening.

She meant to shake her head no, and yet, found herself opening her mouth to receive him.

He stood inches from her, his naked chest just one undone button away. His breath hot and sweet at her forehead. If she tilted her chin...

"Yeah, I do. This one isn't for practice, Patricia."

He kissed her, exploring and teasing all her senses. His hands came to rest on her hips, grinding her against his hard, stiff manhood. She sighed, rising up to meet him, and then he pulled away gently.

"I want you," he said huskily.

Her body responded yes.

"I want..." she said. "I want..."

At last she found the strength to shake her head. No.

"Sam, I don't think it's a good idea."

"Why not? You yourself have said we're sophisticated people. We're both consenting adults. We're friends. We can handle it."

How little he knew. She couldn't handle it, and he wouldn't be able to handle it when he discovered just how inexperienced she was.

"That's just it," she improvised. "We're friends."

"You think this—" he kissed the back of her neck "—will destroy our friendship?"

"I don't know. I don't want to risk it."

"And getting married won't destroy us?"

He brought his head back and stared down at her. She blinked and then looked away.

"Patricia, you're a real mystery. You seem as sure of yourself as any woman could be. But still, every once in a while, I look into your eyes and I see an innocence there that is so at odds with the businesswoman I work with."

"I'm not...innocent," Patricia lied boldly.

"I'd never take advantage of you if you were."

"How do you define an innocent?"

"A virgin. Or a woman who might as well be for lack of experience."

Oh, that was her.

"Is that what you like in a woman—experience?"

"It's just I don't want to be responsible for hurting a woman."

Patricia bit her lips.

"You wouldn't hurt me," she said. "I just don't think we should sleep together. It won't...it won't help at the office. Things are complicated enough."

He let go of her as swiftly as if she had announced that she was a pot of boiling water. The ache left by the absence of his touch brought tears to her eyes.

"I'm sorry, Patricia," he said. "I hate men who use their position at work to make a woman..."

"That's not it. It's just I think I need some space," she said, looking away so that he wouldn't see the torment in her eyes. "This is getting a little intense."

"I'll get my things," he said.

He quickly gathered up his clothes and cuff links. When he was done, she had recovered enough to hold the door for him.

"See you at the office," she said.

"Sure thing," he said, his voice easy while his body was near to exploding. "And again, thank you. If there's anything…"

"There isn't," she said firmly, and closed the door.

Cold shower.

And fast.

Patricia peeled her T-shirt up over her head.

Cold shower.

Now! Before she ran right out that door and begged him to make love to her.

And what would be so wrong about that? she wondered.

She had no idea what to do with a man.

That's what would be so wrong.

Maybe she was a freak.

She got halfway down the hall before she remembered the T-shirt lying on the floor. I'm not Sam, she thought, and went back to pick it up. I still have my standards.

Cold shower.

The urgency was not to be denied by a mere desire to keep her apartment neat and tidy. She dropped the T-shirt and struggled with her jeans all the way down the hall. With one leg in her jeans and one leg out, she set the cold water full blast and remembered that Sam had thrown the only bath towel on the floor by the bed. As she went to get it, she caught sight of herself in the mirror.

I'm not so bad, she thought, putting her hands to her bare waist. A little more curvy at the hips than Kate Moss, but still okay. One foot reflexively shoved her jeans to the floor. She turned to check out the side view and tugged at the waist of her panties. Then she reached her hands up to cup her breasts. They felt full and aching—her nipples were hard and tight against the smooth cup of her bra. She always thought it would have been nice to have a little more up top....

She dropped her hands as if an alarm had gone off.

Which it had.

She shuddered guiltily until she realized it was just the phone.

"Hello, Patricia, it's Mildred again—sorry for the static but the car phone isn't working right. I forgot to tell you that Rex is having a little tea party at his home this afternoon and he thought it would be nice for you and Sam to see the place where you'll be married. Can you come?"

Patricia glanced out the window at Sam as he got into his car.

"Of course, we'd love to," she said quickly. "What time?"

"Four o'clock," Mildred said. "That just gives

you two hours, but I was sure that if you two are practically living together that Sam would still be…"

"Okay, goodbye!"

Patricia cranked open the window and shouted at Sam, but he had already closed the driver's-side door. If she didn't catch up with him, and they missed that tea…!

She ran down the stairs and out to the parking lot, catching up with his car just as he reached the curb. She hopped on one foot and then another, the blacktop scalding her soles. She waved frantically. He looked surprised to see her, even puzzled.

The driver's-side window rolled down.

He tucked his aviator sunglasses down for a good long look.

"What's going on?"

"Mildred called to ask us to tea this afternoon. Four o'clock. That's two hours from now. Should we go?"

He kept staring. And then she noticed. In one horrifying moment she realized that she was standing on the sidewalk in nothing more than her panties, a bra and a blush.

"Why, Miss Peel, we're even," he said, getting out of the car.

"Even?"

He tugged his shirt up over his head and handed it to her.

"I've showed you mine. You've showed me yours. I got the better view."

She would have liked to run. She would have liked to give him, no! *thrown him* back his shirt. She would have liked to wipe that grin off his face. She would have liked to tell him to stop gawking. She would have liked to have the blacktop that was burning beneath her feet do a little more burning; maybe being swallowed up in molten liquid would be nicer than standing here watching his frank appraisal.

And yet she didn't run. Didn't give him back his shirt—and in fact, did nothing with it except crumple it in her arms. Didn't tell him to stop gawking because she was uncertain whether she wanted him to stop.

Did he think she was pretty?

Did he think she was sexy?

Then she heard it.

A wolf whistle from a passing car.

That broke the spell.

She put on his shirt, buttoned it as high as the buttons would allow and tugged it down, covering her hips with a good half inch to spare. Squared her shoulders to a vaguely military stance. Scowled at him.

But still he grinned, crossing his arms over his chest and leaning against his idling car as if he had all the time in the world. If she had been the kind of a woman who let her eyes travel, she would have noticed that his jeans strained against his groin in a most suggestive manner.

And she was the kind of a woman who let her eyes travel.

But when her gaze returned to his, she noticed the gotcha! expression of a man who knows a woman has admired him.

"We have two hours," he said. "We can do a lot with two hours."

"Tea at four o'clock," she said primly. "I would suggest you change."

And she walked back into the apartment building with all the grace and majesty she could summon.

She needed that cold shower.

She needed it bad.

But however badly she needed it, she was pleased to note he needed it worse.

"Good morning, Mrs. McGillicuddy," she said as she passed her landlady sweeping the stairs.

"And I always thought you were such a nice, quiet girl," Mrs. McGillicuddy muttered.

Two hours later when she got into Sam's car, he told her he was just as surprised as her landlady.

"I never knew you were a lace underwear kind of woman," he said when she got into the car.

Patricia wore a whisper-weight floral sundress with pale ivory stockings and a pair of white sandals. There was no way he could see her underwear now.

It was white. And cotton. The kind guaranteed to make her feel asexual.

"I took a cold shower," Patricia said. "The kind with icicles. I take it you didn't do the same."

"No," Sam said. "I drove around Phoenix and Scottsdale for an hour and a half wondering why we weren't making love."

She looked him up and down. He wore khakis with a pale yellow oxford button-down shirt and a blue silk knit tie. His hair was neatly combed, his face smooth and tan.

"I had just enough time for a quick shower and shave so I could pick you up," he explained. "Patricia, I want to make love to you."

"I know," she said, worrying the straw handle of her purse.

"And I know you do, too. At least, I can feel you do."

She didn't answer.

"All right, maybe I'm wrong," he said. "It's just me that's feeling this tension. But it's there for me. I want you. I've never paid attention to you as anything other than a friend and a colleague. But right now, Patricia, I'd give anything to take you upstairs to your apartment and rip that sundress off you and make love to you for hours and hours."

"And miss Rex's tea party?"

"Hours and hours." Sam nodded.

Her heart soared. This was everything she had ever wanted. He noticed her. He saw her. He wanted her. And although the cold shower had done wonders, fire had started back up within her. She'd like to tell him yes. Take me upstairs. Make love to me within an inch of my life.

But first I have to tell you this itsy-bitsy little secret about me....

I don't know what I'm doing, Sam, I need you to show me how.

"I won't do this again," Sam said. "You're full of surprises, but I know this much about you— you're not the kind of woman who can have an affair with a man just for kicks. And I'm not the kind of man who can offer you anything more."

"Well, then, I guess that settles it, don't you think?" she asked.

"Yeah, I guess it does," he said, looking not the least bit settled.

She closed her eyes as he started the engine. It was as if a door had been slammed in her face. But she rallied her dignity, and by the time the butler at the Hacienda Barrington announced Mr. Sam Wainwright and his fiancée, Patricia Peel, she was all smiles—as any blushing bride-to-be should be.

Chapter Twelve

The first thing that dropped on Patricia's desk was a pair of red silk boxer shorts. Followed by a house key. Then an electric razor. In more rapid succession, a black toothbrush, a mesh University of Arizona basketball jersey and a peach negligee with a matching maribou-trimmed robe.

Patricia looked up from the spreadsheet on employee benefits that had baffled her all morning.

This baffled her even more.

"He bought me the night set," Melissa explained haughtily. She tapped a pale pink manicured finger on Patricia's desk. "Well, at least he did when I told him to. I've decided I don't like the color. It's spring and I'm a winter."

"Winter?"

"My coloring is winter."

Patricia nodded, although she had scant idea of what Melissa was talking about.

"I'm a winter and winters need dramatic colors," Melissa continued. "Peach looks good on me, but not as good as other colors do. So I'm returning it."

"Naturally."

"Along with all his other stuff."

Melissa then dropped a grass-stained baseball and a wooden bat on top of the pile and wiped her hands together briskly.

"That's it," she said. "I'm all done with Sam Wainwright. It's as if he never existed."

"What about the emeralds?"

Melissa gulped and touched her earlobes—twin emeralds twinkled guiltily in beds of tiny matching diamonds.

"What emeralds?"

"Sam got you emerald earrings for Valentine's Day. Those emeralds, as a matter of fact."

"You're such a detail-oriented person," Melissa shot back. "No wonder you have a job here. Well, I'm keeping them. The best etiquette books say that a woman can keep any gifts that a man gave her during courtship. Especially when emeralds look this good on me."

"Don't worry. Sam doesn't care. He'd let you have them. He'd probably only be concerned about getting back his ball and bat. I don't know about the peach negligee."

"All I'm really obligated to give him is the engagement ring, and I notice you have my ring on your hand.''

Melissa leaned over the desk, bringing an overpowering draft of Chanel No. 5 with her. She grabbed Patricia's hand and examined the ring.

''It's mine now,'' Patricia said in a voice that came out a lot smaller than she would have liked.

''Hope you have better luck than me.'' Melissa sniffed.

''What do you mean?''

''He's not capable of loving a woman,'' Melissa said with certainty. She dropped Patricia's hand. ''He is always keeping part of himself back.''

Patricia knew she shouldn't ask, but she couldn't stop herself.

''Is that why you broke up?''

''It's certainly not because I did anything wrong.''

Patricia leaned over the spreadsheet and offered Melissa a seat and a cup of coffee. Melissa accepted the former and declined the latter.

''What do you think he wants in a woman?'' Patricia asked. ''What did he like?''

Melissa sat down, smoothing her red silk shantung skirt over her gym-toned thighs. She put her chin in one hand, and Patricia would look back on that moment and swear that steam came out of Melissa's ears as she used every neuron in thinking out her reply.

''He liked me in silk. He liked me in pearls. He

liked me in lace. He liked me in nothing at all. Hey, why are you asking me?''

''I just want to know from your perspective.''

Melissa stared hard.

''Sister, you've got it bad. Sam's a wonderful lover. The best. We both know that,'' she said, little noticing the flicker of hurt that passed across Patricia's face. ''But when he's made love to you—made every one of your senses explode with joy, there's still something missing, isn't there? And that's the feeling that he's opened himself up to you.''

Melissa took a moment from reflecting upon her own troubles to glance at Patricia.

''Darling, you've never made love to him, have you?''

''I don't have to answer that.''

''You don't need to,'' she said. Then she added in a whisper, ''Listen, he's a lot of man. With a man's appetites. A woman has to be mighty strong to stand up to him and to give him what he wants.''

Patricia gulped.

''He needs a real woman,'' Melissa concluded.

''And you weren't...?''

''That wasn't the problem,'' Melissa shot back, turning a shade of pink that neatly matched her suit. ''I wouldn't have married him anyway. He wasn't civilized enough.''

''Really?''

''Has no family money. Self-made man. It's a very attractive quality at the beginning of a court-ship. And a tiring one at the end. My daddy's sending me to Europe to forget him. Now you can do me an itsy-bitsy little favor before I go.''

"I'm thrilled. What is it?''

"I don't want to meet up with Sam. Too hard in the dignity department. Could you check his office and see if there's a picture of me on his desk? If there is, I want it back.''

"Okay, but stay here. And don't try to decipher these spreadsheets.''

"I wouldn't dream of it. I find math to be really yucky.''

Patricia walked down the hallway to Sam's office. If she had been thinking, she could have told Melissa that he was out at a conference on pension benefits programs and wouldn't be back until lunchtime. She could get her own picture. A check of his desk and the file credenza revealed no picture of Melissa.

In fact, the only picture was a sterling framed five-by-seven of Patricia taken when they were interviewing students at Fort Lauderdale last spring. It hadn't been there before today. She looked happy—even if her nose and cheeks were the color of a cactus rose.

It made her smile.

He's just putting it there until it's time to get a divorce, a warning voice inside her purred.

"Yeah, but at least it's here,'' she said aloud.

"Sorry, no pictures,'' Patricia said as she stepped back into her office. "Hey, have you been trying to understand those spreadsheets?''

Melissa looked up from Patricia's desk—and held her hand over the receiver of the phone.

"It's your mother," she explained. "Why didn't you tell her you were getting married?"

Patricia smacked her forehead as Melissa picked up her purse, waved cheerily and left the office.

"Mom…"

"I'm coming for the wedding."

"No, Mom, it's not that kind of wedding," Patricia said, leaning backward to kick the door of her office closed. She didn't want anyone overhearing this conversation. "It's not that kind of marriage."

"What do you mean? My only daughter getting married. I have to come."

"Mom, do you remember when you and father were stationed in Russia when it was still the Soviet Union and there was that physicist they were going to send to Siberia?"

"Yes, I seem to recall your father's secretary married Sergei Rathmikolov so he could be given diplomatic immunity and smuggled to the United States."

"Right. It's like that."

"The secretary divorced him," Mrs. Peel continued. "As soon as he was safely in the States. He got a fellowship at Harvard—but that was an arranged marriage."

"Right, and Mother, this marriage is just—"

"Although she, of course, could never return to the Soviet Union," her mother interrupted. "So your father found her a job in Paraguay just before he died.''

''Well, this is just like that.''

There was a long pause.

''Mom. Mom. Are you still there?''

''Oh, dear,'' Mrs. Peel said at last. ''Patricia, I never knew Arizona had such political problems. What are you going to do—smuggle him to Texas?''

''Rex gave us these for tonight,'' Sam said, dropping two tickets on Patricia's desk. ''Opera—*Madame Butterfly*.''

''At the Orpheum.'' Patricia sighed blissfully, examining the tickets. ''Isn't that the recently restored theater?''

''It's very nice. Gilded staircase and all.''

''I'd like to go,'' Patricia said. ''And it says here we have box seats. Unless, of course, it's too much. We could say that with the wedding coming up, we have so much to do…''

''These are Rex's tickets. He was supposed to greet the governor this evening—the governor will be in the adjoining box. I've agreed to say hello on Rex's behalf. It would look quite odd if you didn't go with me.''

''I don't have a thing to wear.''

''Don't wear anything,'' Sam teased. He dodged a playful slap. ''What you're wearing now looks pretty good.''

She wore a coral silk shantung suit with a bitter-lemon-colored shell. Her hair was just that right balance between tousled and tamed—she had to wake up forty-five minutes earlier each morning to get the right effect, and her arms ached from pointing the blow-dryer with one hand while wielding the rounded brush in the other.

But try as she might, she knew she'd have ink stains and wrinkles on her suit and her hair would have curled and kinked of its own accord by curtain time at the Orpheum.

"These are work clothes," Patricia said. "I'll wear a gown."

Her checking account balance was dipping close to zero but, with Gascon as her adviser, she had a dress for every occasion.

"Whatever happened to all your gray suits and white high-collared blouses?"

"I'm trying not to look dowdy," Patricia said.

"You never looked dowdy. But you look hot now. I noticed last night at dinner that you got your share of male attention. Who was that man who stopped at the table and asked for your autograph?"

"He was a fan of Elizabeth Shue," Patricia said. "He seemed quite upset that I wrote Patricia Peel on his cocktail napkin."

"I should be jealous."

"Are you?"

"Of course not," Sam said, little noticing the way her shoulders dropped. "By the way, you smell nice, too."

"I do? I mean, thank you."

"Yeah, you smell like…"

"An intoxicating blend of Oriental spices?" she asked hopefully. She had shelled out a little less than a hundred dollars for an ounce of the precious stuff. But the sales lady assured her that men were helpless with desire when they sniffed a woman with this perfume on.

She had not yet found a perfume that advertised that men's voracious sexual interest would be turned into love. When she did, she planned to bring a gallon jug and say "Fill 'er up."

He had promised he would never compromise her again.

And that was a promise he had delivered on, to her frustration and to her relief. He joked, he complimented, he admired, he whistled on occasion, he even lingered in his admiring glance.

But he never stepped over the line to seduction.

Patricia had no doubt that if she crooked her finger, he would take her. Take her and satisfy her.

And the prospect scared her senseless.

So the past two weeks had been perfectly chaste. She sensed he was interested in her, beyond the bounds of friendship. But Sam was, to quote Melissa, "a lot of man...with a man's appetite." He wanted to make love. It took every bit of her self-control to say no when her body wanted so badly to say yes.

But if she said yes, he'd know she was an innocent. And then she'd lose him.

Sam leaned forward, nearly touching her cheek with his nose.

"No, that's not perfume. It's the chocolate croissant. Are you going to eat that?"

"Here," she said, pushing the pastry across her desk. "I shouldn't eat it anyway. Mildred says I can't gain or lose an ounce before the wedding or my dress won't fit."

"Shouldn't be hard for you," he said, biting into her croissant.

"Especially if you're eating my breakfast."

He stood up, flicking a last crumb of the croissant off his lapel.

"Are you sure you don't mind going to the opera? I've been keeping you out late nearly every night."

It had been a whirlwind week and a half since Rex's retirement party. Everyone wanted to entertain the newly engaged couple. Late nights and early mornings to play catch-up at the office didn't make for a lot of introspection about the deceit they were really engaged in.

"I'll be okay. If Rex wanted to say hi to the governor, he must have a reason."

"Great. Because there isn't anybody else I'd be willing to go with. Melissa took me once—I fell asleep and she got really mad. Pick you up at eight."

"Sure thing."

He tossed her a kiss. It was three whole seconds before Mike the mailman came in with her mail and Patricia realized the kiss had only been for show. There had been a lot of those kind of kisses—and a few extra for good measure—in the past two weeks.

"Hey, Patricia, here's your mail," Mike said. "You're looking a little down. Wedding jitters?"

"Oh, no," Patricia said, shaking her head. "Er, maybe that's it."

"It's awfully nice of Mr. Barrington to give you a wedding."

"It sure is. But it's too bad that his son the Third won't be coming."

"The Third?"

"Yeah, we call Rex the Second's son the Third. Because he's Rex Barrington the Third. Get it?"

Mike's handsome face broke out into a grin.

"Got it. Why isn't he coming?"

"Business. He's been assigned out of the country for what seems like forever. No one's ever seen him. Except Rex the Second, of course."

Mike laughed.

"By the way," he said, pushing the mail cart farther down the hall. "I'm supposed to tell you that your mother is here."

"Here?" Patricia gulped. "Where here?"

"In the lobby. Waiting for you. See ya later, Patricia."

Chapter Thirteen

Patricia shoved her feet into high heels—the ones so high that she could barely walk in them. But this morning she could sprint. All the way to the elevator bank, and when the elevator didn't come fast enough, down the stairs to the glass-enclosed lobby. Her mother, regally clad in an aquamarine suit with a fuchsia blouse, stood talking to the receptionist.

"Mother, what are you doing here?" Patricia asked.

Her mother rushed to greet her.

"Bon matin!" she cried out, seeming to forget that Americans, her daughter included, didn't always speak French.

"Mother, it's wonderful to see you, but what are you doing here?" Patricia repeated, softening her voice as she noticed the receptionist peering over her copy of a glamour magazine.

"I'm here for my only daughter's wedding," Mrs. Peel said. "Even if it is just a marriage for legal purposes."

"Mother!"

Her mother looked over at the receptionist.

"I don't think she approves of me," Mrs. Peel whispered to Patricia. "Listen, you're getting married day after tomorrow and I wouldn't miss it for the world. Besides, immigration officials would take note of the fact that the mother of the bride didn't appear at the wedding. It would count against you.... Oh, dear, Patricia."

"What?"

"You're in love," her mother said, with the same tone of voice she would have used to announce the end of the world.

"How do you know?"

"I can see it in your eyes."

Patricia touched her brow bone.

"Does it show?" she asked, grimacing when her mother nodded. If her mother could see, so could the world. "No, you can't see a thing."

"Patricia, a mother knows these things. Even a mother who hasn't spent much time with her daughter. You're marrying for love, and he's not—that's the real problem, isn't it?"

"Please, Mom, keep your voice down," Patricia said, hustling her mother into an elevator. "I've got to get you to my office. You're going to stay there and not get into any trouble."

"I never get into trouble."

"That's what you said before that incident in Helsinki."

For the first time in Patricia's memory, her mother didn't launch into an explanation of how Helsinki was all the government's fault.

Patricia escorted her mother into her office and shut the door behind them. Then she sat with her mother on the love seat by the window and told her…everything. And yet she found herself glossing over the parts that had to do with her virginity. She just couldn't confess that to her mother!

"I love him," she concluded. "But I know he doesn't love me. Yet. Is getting married to him so terrible?"

"I'm hardly in the position to pass judgment," her mother said. "I only wish that Sam could see what a wonderful woman you are. And how precious your love for him is."

She reached out to touch the lapel of Patricia's silk suit.

"Funny, this is exactly the sort of beautiful, dramatic outfit I always wanted you to wear. Your makeup and hair is more polished and sophisticated. You're even in heels, and that perfume is so French! Why, you've even stopped biting your nails."

"Have to. You can't bite acrylic tips."

"After all these years of my nagging you to get some glamour and some sexiness, you finally do it."

"You like it?"

"Yes, of course."

"No you don't," Patricia said.

"Okay. Call me crazy, but I miss the old Patricia. I miss the ponytail. The freckles. The chewed-to-the-quick nails. I must be losing my mind—I'm even feeling nostalgic for your gray suits. It wasn't chic. But it was you.''

"I'm making myself over because I want Sam to notice me. To fall in love with me. He wouldn't if I didn't make some changes.''

"Is Sam really so shallow that a little eye shadow, a flashy dress and a manicure is going to make him head over heels?''

"No, but I want to be his kind of woman. To be his colleague, friend, lover and his wife.''

"Oh, my dear daughter, you've got it bad, but he's got it worse.''

"What do you mean—he's got it worse?''

"It's difficult enough to love someone so much that you'd do anything for them. But it's a real tragedy to have someone love you that much and you can't even see it.''

It had come down to this: champagne and white roses, tulle and lace, a white duck canvas tent in the backyard of Hacienda Barrington to shield the guests from the unblinking optimism of the late-summer sun. At the French doors leading to the flag-stone courtyard, Mildred Van Hess gave Patricia the abundant bouquet of white desert roses.

"You're doing the right thing,'' she said, and fluttered her hand in the direction of the aisle. "Go on, get going, it's show time.''

The string quartet began to play the bridal march. And Patricia's mother, seated in the first row, had already borrowed a second handkerchief from someone seated behind her. She loudly and dramatically sobbed.

It wasn't until Patricia was halfway down the aisle, having passed Olivia and Rachel—who gave her a buoyant thumbs-up—before she realized what an odd comment Mildred had made.

You're doing the right thing?

What kind of thing is that to say to a bride?

What did she mean by that?

But when Patricia looked back at Mildred, standing at the door in her sorbet-pink suit, the older woman just nodded.

You're doing the right thing?

Patricia looked ahead to the altar, draped with white canvas cloth, and then she saw Sam, his gray eyes steadily focused on her. He wore a white dinner jacket and black slacks. He looked every inch the proud bridegroom.

She had done her best to make him proud. Her dress was a slip of white silk with a barely there chiffon smoke tied at its bodice with crisscrossing ribbons. Gascon had worked his magic with a upsweep of curls—Patricia had vetoed his suggestion that her hair would look best au naturel.

Patricia reached out and squeezed her mother's hand as she approached the altar—and then she took Sam's hand.

''You don't have to...'' he whispered as he took her arm.

She silenced him with a whisper-slight toss of her head.

The minister began the familiar words of the wedding ceremony. She had, as a diplomat's daughter, heard those same words many times—in Greek, in Russian, in Swahili, in Hindu. And yet, spoken here for her benefit, the words carried their own power.

All the work that Mildred had put into this day— the flowers, the champagne, the ribbons hanging from every folding chair—all of it dropped away, leaving only the beauty of a woman, a man and a promise.

She heard the words at first with sadness, realizing how little they truly applied to her. How she wished she was like other women—other women who found their love and would hear these words with confidence and joy. But as the minister continued to read from his book, Patricia felt an odd calm wash over her. And the weeks of deception dropped away.

These words did apply to her. They were the truth. She was entering into some kind of connection to Sam that would exist long after she left Barrington, long after he thanked her and went on with his life—so long, in fact, that there could only be one word for what she was promising. Lifelong marriage. There was no other man whom she could love, whom she could honor, whom she could cherish and

whom she would stand by...in sickness and in
health, in good times and bad.

She would be his bride forever, though he would
think it would end with a divorce. And it would end,
for everyone but herself.

Sam stood stiffly at Patricia's side. He'd never
been to a wedding where he paid attention to the
ceremony. Usually he was the guy outside, tying
cans to the back of the limousine or baby-sitting
impatient flower girls and restless ring bearers.

The sacred words were direct and pointed.

Love. Honor. Cherish.

In sickness and in health. For richer for poorer.
Good times and bad.

'Til death do us part.

Sam's parents had never married. His father
hadn't bothered giving his son his name. And his
mother was too meek to protest the many other
women of Sam's father's life. Sam had decided
early on that he would marry, but this was not a
romantic decision, it was a mark of his determina-
tion to live by the rules of the haves so that he would
never be mistaken for a have-not.

But this wasn't marriage.

Was it?

He glanced back at Rex, who had a smile on his
face as wide as the Rio Grande. He winked at Sam
and Sam smiled in return. He noticed Mildred
threading her arm under Rex's elbow. And Mike the
mail room guy standing on the other side of Rex.

Sam didn't know the full story of Rex's hiring of Mike, but he figured that Mike was like him—a hard-luck case plucked off the streets and given a chance at Barrington Corporation. When Patricia had asked him about why Rex had hired Mike, Sam had been forced to confess he had no idea.

Sam had done well with his chance—adding hard work, persistence and rock-solid fear of failure to the opportunity Rex had given him.

He squeezed Patricia's small hand. She was doing him such a favor. Saving him when he needed saving most. A good friend does that, he thought, but the words of the marriage ceremony went beyond friendship.

She was promising before God that she would be his...forever. And he was doing the same. It was wrong to play with the sacred ceremony this way.

He should stop it now.

Tell everyone gathered here that this was a sham marriage, that he was a fraud, a fake, an outsider to their kind.

That he was nothing more than a street-tough barrio boy who had made it to the executive suites. But perhaps he didn't belong here and now was the time to admit it.

When Rex wanted the stability of Sam married, he wanted the wrong-side-of-the-tracks part of Sam tamed. And try as Sam might, perhaps it wasn't tamed.

Because he couldn't love a woman. Couldn't give everything to her. Couldn't give it to Melissa. And here he was playacting at giving his love to the best friend he'd ever had.

And yet, now that he was here, there was no graceful exit, no way that wouldn't humiliate Patricia.

He admired her. Stood in awe of her willingness to give everything to a friend. She was a beauty and would make a man a wonderful wife someday. She deserved the very best....

What does she want? a street-smart voice inside him demanded. A quick promotion? A salary boost? A better job? A good reference? Or simply the promise that she would always follow his star as it rose into the corporate stratosphere?

No, she's doing this because she...thinks of me as a friend, he thought.

He wondered if he deserved a friend as good as Patricia, but he never had the time to explore the answer to that self-query. The minister had told him, for the second time, that he could kiss the bride.

She looked up at him with such radiant innocence that he nearly blurted out that he was a jerk, a first-rate jerk who had taken this woman's offer of friendship and turned it inside out.

But her smile, so Mona Lisa, so filled with mystery and beauty, gave him pause. She laid a hand on the lapel of his white dinner jacket.

With that touch, as powerful as a magician's wand, he forgot everything about himself.

He kissed her. And promised with the touch of his lips upon hers that he was her man. Forever. And all the other words the minister had asked him to repeat.

Her mouth opened, surrendering to him.

Her head leaned back. He felt the unsteadiness of her posture and steadied her with his hand at the small of her back. He tasted the lips, now somewhat familiar because of the very public kisses they had exchanged. But something new happened when he touched his tongue to her smooth teeth—she opened to him. He plunged his tongue into her mouth, taking her rich velvety flesh for his own.

When he came up for air, they were both shell-shocked.

"Ladies and gentlemen, it is my pleasure to present Mr. and Mrs. Sam Wainwright," the minister announced with a grin.

The guests erupted with applause that nearly, but not quite, drowned out Mrs. Peel blowing her nose.

Sam walked down the aisle with Patricia, and the caterer met them with two glasses of champagne.

"Every time they give a toast, you have to kiss the bride," he warned Sam.

"Sure," Sam said, feeling such happiness that he didn't even second-guess himself.

Chapter Fourteen

There was a toast and then another. Kisses and then more. Sam felt as heady as if he had gotten the chance to finish his glass of champagne, which of course he didn't because just as he would kiss Patricia to satisfy the clamor of well-wishers, he would be asked to kiss her again.

He wanted to take her and repeat every kiss in private.

How he suffered through a dinner of chicken mole and balsamic rice he could never say. Or cutting the cake and licking the icing from Patricia's mouth but going no further. Shaking hands with a hundred people whose faces blurred in the light of the sinking sun.

Question: How did he manage to tap his heels at the side of the flagstone patio as Rex danced the very first dance with Patricia? Answer: Impatiently.

And when the mountain air grew cool and sweet—well, as cool as Arizona in August allows—how did he stop himself from just hoisting her up over his shoulder like a caveman and taking her home?

Just weeks ago, he would have considered the notion of kissing the assistant personnel director of Barrington Corporation perfectly silly. Just weeks ago, dancing with her would have carried as much spark as the mandatory sixth grade square dance lessons he suffered through. Just weeks ago, Patricia Peel figured in his daydream—to the extent that he had them—as a minor figure with whom he shared some business accolade.

Now her kisses were as irresistible as chocolate, her laughter as precious as diamonds and her skin as touchable as silk.

He liked her. Always had. Thought she was a good sport, a team player, a fun gal to be around.

Now he lusted after her.

At midnight, he told her they were going, as they danced to the string quartet's medley of Harry Connick, Jr. songs.

"Home?" she asked, blinking twice.

"Yes, home. Patricia, I want you," he murmured, feeling his groin tighten as he confessed. "I think you want me, too."

She stared at him, the dark brown of her dark pupils expanding so that all that remained of the Irish in her was a slim line of jade. Then she blinked, dropped her head and looked away.

"Yes, I do," she said softly. "I do."

The next few minutes were chaotic. Rex shook Patricia's hand, joyful tears streaming down his face, and then kissed Sam on the cheek—and promptly apologized for being so confused that he reversed his course and kissed Patricia's cheek and gave a jolly handshake to his vice president. Mildred gave Patricia the bouquet to throw and Sophia, the new assistant to the Third, caught it. Sam glanced over at Mike and gave him a thumbs-up, though he knew that Sophia at least claimed not to be interested in the mail room guy.

As the couple walked out to the courtyard where his car awaited, Mildred handed each guest a pyramid-shaped box, and at her direction, the hundred boxes were opened. A delicate canopy of butterflies flittered first toward the spotlights that illuminated Rex's hacienda and then toward the dark mountain peaks.

A hundred shouted goodbyes followed Sam and Patricia all the way down the drive to the wrought-iron gates of Hacienda Barrington.

They didn't speak in the car. Sam didn't want to spoil the moment. But when they pulled into his driveway, he jumped out of the car and got to the passenger's-side door before she could open it.

"Allow me," he said, and he picked her up in his arms and carried her into the house.

When he flipped on the hallway light, he noticed her face was flushed, upturned to him as if she had made herself into a gift for him. The kisses of a hundred wedding toasts had done their magic.

"I want you," he said huskily, feeling thick in his throat. "I want you, Patricia."

He put his arms out to embrace her, but she backed away. He felt a sudden quickening of his nerves, as if the two glasses of champagne were swept out of his system and replaced with high-voltage java.

"Sam, there's two things I should tell you."

He glanced up.

"If it's about birth control, I already..."

"No, it's not," she said. Her face was stricken with sadness.

"Oh, no," he said, and leaned back against the console table. "You don't want to make love to me."

"I do. I really do. But I should tell you..."

"First," he prompted, and waited. Here it would finally come, when he desired her so badly that he would even get down on his knees.

Perhaps she meant to ask something of him, something important; whatever it was, he would give it to her. Even as her request would confirm, once and for all, that everybody did things for a reason, with an expectation of a payback.

"First thing is...I'm a virgin."

He faltered, stepping back and nearly losing his balance until he realized he had never even managed a sip of the wedding champagne. It was shock that nearly toppled him. He hadn't expected this. And yet, the moment she said it, he realized all the signs had been there.

"A virgin?"

She nodded, chin at her collarbone, her hair tumbling in front of her face.

He had done wrong—he had taken her higher and higher, and she didn't even know where she was, how close she was to losing that most precious gift of womanhood. Her cheeks were red, her eyes dark as night and her breasts swelled and strained against the gauzy fabric, her nipples stiff. And unconsciously she rubbed one thigh against the inside of the other.

"Oh, man," he muttered, and he sat down on the second stair leading up to his bedroom. "And what's the second thing?"

He stood back up and came to her. He knew he had not just brought a woman to the brink, but he had taken the heart of his best friend. She was in love.

"Don't tell me," he whispered. "Please don't tell me. I think I already know."

She tugged her floral wreath off her head.

"So now you know my one terrible secret. And you probably can guess my second terrible secret."

He brought her chin up with a gentle finger.

"Not so terrible."

"Which one's not terrible? Being a freak of nature at twenty-nine…"

"Being a virgin doesn't make you a freak."

She ignored him, blinking back tears.

"I never should have gotten you into this."

"You didn't know. I didn't tell you. I was ashamed and worried that you'd think less of me."

He rubbed his jaw.

"A woman's virginity is a precious gift."

"I'm ready to give it to you, and you don't look like a kid on Christmas morning."

He put his arms around her. She felt the quickening of hope, but then faltered as he kept a decorous three inches between them.

"No, I won't take advantage of you," he said.

"I'm asking you to," she replied. Her aching need for him was making her reckless and bold.

He shook his head.

"I'm not that kind of man," he said. "I'll go make up the bedroom for you."

"Where are you going to sleep?"

"The couch."

The gently delivered words were nonetheless as painful as a knife. She kicked off her peau de soie heels. Fumbled with a hairpin that scraped the back of her neck. Wiped away a tear with the back of her hand, not even caring that her lipstick and eye shadow smudged into a big purple stain.

She went upstairs. He was making the bed.

"I admit it, Sam. I hoped if we spent a lot of time together—pretending to be a couple—that you'd take a look at me and decide that I was..."

"Was what?" He looked up.

"Pretty enough. Smart enough. Lovable enough."

"Oh, Patricia. You always were those things."

"But you didn't notice."

"You're right. But maybe I'm not the kind of man you should have noticing you. Oh, Patricia, you did this all because you hoped I'd fall in love with you?"

"That wasn't the only reason I did it. I just plain want the best for you, enough that I'd do anything to help you get the happiness you want."

"Even if nothing was given to you in return? Even if I'm telling you that I'm not the kind of man who loves a woman completely? Even if I'm saying my career and my ambitions will always come first?"

She nodded.

He countered with an emphatic shake of his head.

"If it ended right here, Patricia, would it have been worth it?"

"If you got to keep the job you love, yes," she said without hesitation. "Sam, I don't think this has to change anything. We're still going to get a divorce when Rex is happily settled on his tour and your job is secure."

"I think it changes everything," Sam said. "I've taken advantage of someone. No, not just someone. I've taken advantage of a friend…my best friend."

"You didn't take advantage of me," she said, reaching across the bed, but he stepped back. "I knew what I was doing."

He shook his head emphatically.

"You haven't had enough experience in life to

know what you're doing. You're like a kid playing with matches. You didn't mean to get burned but you did. We both did. Now get some sleep. We'll figure out what to do in the morning."

"I'm still going to give you the divorce when the time comes," she said, using the back of her hand to wipe away the tears that just wouldn't stop coming. "I'm still going to do everything we agreed on. And I won't regret it. Not one little bit. Because I did it for you. Oh, that's not true. I did it for me. I did it...for us."

He paused at the door.

"Patricia, you're the only woman I trust well enough to know that you would do what you said you'd do. But you're also the one woman I wouldn't want to ask."

As he gently closed the door behind him, Patricia slumped onto the bed.

Why did I tell him about my being a virgin? she asked herself.

Because he would have known.

If they had made love, he would have known.

And all the fancy hairdos, new clothes and heels wouldn't have made any difference. She was a simple woman with simple tastes, looks that pulled her fair share of male attention but not a smidgen more, and experience in sex that was little enough to get her a place in the *Guinness Book of World Records*.

She pulled apart an acrylic tip, wincing as it peeled off the slim natural nail bed. Then she did another. And another.

When she had her nails back down to normal, she combed her hair out, put it in a scrunchie and fished a T-shirt and panties from the bottom of the suitcase she had packed for the two-day honeymoon Mildred had planned at the Barrington Spa in New Mexico. She scrubbed off her makeup, saying hello to the freckles that had become almost unfamiliar in the past two weeks. She scoured her wrists and neck of the expensive perfume—the clean smell of soap wasn't seductive, but it was her.

She got under the covers, inhaling the scent of him on his bed.

It was too much.

She came downstairs and found him sitting on the couch, holding a snifter of brandy in one hand, the other hand tightly bound in a fist.

"Sam, I'm not going to be able to sleep," she said. "Will you please come to bed with me?"

He looked up at her. Dark lines of worry criss-crossed his forehead.

"I won't make love to you."

"I'm not asking that. I'm asking for something much more difficult."

His jaws throbbed and then he nodded. He put down the glass and followed her upstairs. He pulled off his tie and belt, allowing himself the top button on his shirt undone. Then he got into bed and as gently as he would cradle one of the butterflies that Mildred had flown in from out East, he held Patricia in his arms.

She didn't sleep, even as later she heard his

breathing grow deep and still. His arms felt heavy around her, but she didn't budge. She had never shared a bed with a man, but she didn't get out to find a more comfortable place to sleep. Instead, she watched the glow-in-the-dark clock on the dresser. Three o'clock, four o'clock, five. And she waited until it was a decent hour to call Mildred to explain that she had to leave Barrington.

"Morning, Sam. Here's your mail," Mike said, pushing his cart into Sam's office. "That Parisian company sent you a jumbo-size sample box of their perfumed soaps they hope you'll use in the Antigua and Bahamas resorts. I'll bring it up later. I'll also let you in on a secret. The soaps start off with a fine, subtle scent, but then they leave an 'aftersmell' like day-old eggs."

Sam looked up from his paperwork. How would Mike the mailman know how the most expensive soaps made in Europe would smell?

"Hey, aren't you supposed to be on a honeymoon?" Mike asked. "And what should a groom be doing the morning after his wedding?"

"Catching up on paperwork," Sam guessed.

"Staying in bed. Besides, it's so early!"

Real early. But not so early that Patricia wasn't already gone. He called her apartment and got no answer. He'd get these few last matters wrapped up, have a talk with Rex that he didn't look forward to and go back home and find her. Somehow he'd have to find her and make her realize that he had done wrong. Very wrong.

"You know, Mike, you've made a good choice working in the mail room," Sam said.

Mike looked up from his sorting of Sam's inter-office deliveries.

"I have?"

"If you put your career ahead of everything else, it's so easy to think that getting ahead is important enough to lose friends, to lose a good woman over."

"Aw, don't be so hard on yourself. As a mail room employee, I can tell you women don't give you a chance."

"You're thinking of Sophia? I've noticed your interest in her hasn't diminished."

"Is it that obvious?"

"Yeah."

"She wants a man with a corner office, a secretary and a stock option plan. She wouldn't want a man without those essential qualities."

Mike rolled his cart out of the office.

Sam signed a few letters, returned a couple of phone calls and then adjusted his tie and put on his suit jacket. Then he walked down the empty halls of the Barrington Corporation.

He didn't need to call ahead—Rex would be in his office. After all, Sam had come down the hall many early mornings, before the rest of the company got to work. Sometimes to talk about issues related to business, sometimes just to analyze the previous evening's pro basketball game and sometimes just to share a cup of coffee.

"Aren't you supposed to be on a honeymoon?" Mildred asked, looking up from her filing as Sam entered Rex's spacious office.

"Where can I find Rex?"

"He'll be in later," Mildred said, shoving her face back into her work. "Have a seat."

Sam sat on the leather tufted couch by the window. Mildred whistled an excruciatingly happy tune while scrutinizing some blueprints.

"It was a wonderful wedding," Mildred said, shoving the blueprints into the back of the file cabinet. "Even if I did plan it myself. The butterflies were just spectacular. Wouldn't you agree?"

"You did a great job," Sam said soberly. "The butterflies were great. And they all lived."

"And that cake!" Mildred exclaimed, oblivious to his discomfort. "I don't mind telling you that I'm going to have to spend extra hours on the Stair-Master to make up for that indulgence. That champagne was marvelous—oooh! My head hurts just a little this morning. You don't look so good yourself."

He reluctantly met her gaze.

"It's nothing I can't recover from."

"Still, wonderful wedding. And after such a long courtship. Rex was talking about how pleased he was that you got engaged months ago. But he could never remember the name of your intended. Never even suspected it was you and Patricia. You two were so discreet. Yes, a wedding after a long court-ship is very satisfying.''

Sam nodded, wondering when he could cut into her chatter to ask when she thought Rex was coming in.

Mildred pulled off her glasses.

''Or was it a short courtship?''

Sam swallowed. Hard.

''I overheard some of the girls from the lunch-room talking about how it was just last week that Patricia was bemoaning the fact that you'd never noticed her,'' Mildred said, staring at him over her reading glasses. ''That she was going to pull to-gether her courage and tell you her feelings. And this was just before Rex invited your fiancée to his retirement party. Which is it, Sam? Long or short? Whirlwind courtship or slowly developing relation-ship?''

Sam closed his eyes and took a deep breath.

''How long have you known the truth?''

''From the very beginning.''

''How?''

''Patricia was wearing the same ring that Melissa Stanhope was photographed displaying in last month's issue of *Phoenix Life*. You forget I like gos-sip. Even if I do know when to keep a secret.''

''Speaking of secrets—Rex?''

She smiled smugly.

''What he doesn't know won't hurt him.''

''I have to tell him.''

''I wouldn't advise it.''

"Why not?"

"Because I'm not sure that until you know what the truth is you should try to explain it to Rex."

"The truth is I married Patricia because I didn't want to disappoint Rex or make him think I wasn't stable enough to keep my job."

"I guess that's at least part of it."

"And the truth is that she married me because she loves me and she wanted the best for me—while at the same time she hoped I would fall in love with her."

Mildred nodded smugly.

"Sounds about right."

"So what am I missing?"

"You're missing the part about how you love Patricia."

"No, Mildred, you're a nice woman. Very sweet. But you've got this wrong. Patricia loves me. It was never the other way around."

Mildred stared heavenward.

"Puh-leeeeze! I might be old but I'm still playing with all my marbles. Sam, give this some thought. Some real, soul-searching thought. And do it quick. Give yourself two or three minutes. Max."

"What's the rush?"

"Patricia called me at home this morning and told me she's resigning. Didn't tell me why, but I made some good guesses. I'm filing her resignation here, under 'things not to be shown to Rex unless absolutely necessary.'"

"Where is she now?" Sam demanded, already halfway down the hall.

"She and her mother are catching the next flight out of here," Mildred called out. "She's leaving. For good."

Chapter Fifteen

Sitting on his porch at sunset. Fishing on the Red River. Basketball at the Scottsdale YMCA. Climbing the face of the canyon. His job, from which he took so much of his identity, and the certain respect of Rex II.

The things he was going to miss about Phoenix because he'd have to leave. Let it be her town. It was the only right thing to do.

He added fifteen to the speed limit, adding another five when traffic was looser. He was banking on Patricia packing everything she had at her apartment, the apartment filled with years of memories and treasures.

It would take a long time.

He didn't know what he would do if she was already gone.

He'd miss Patricia when he left Phoenix. He'd

miss her impossibly proper gray suits. He'd miss the way, even when she was in the middle of a serious discussion, her fingers unconsciously tried to get her hair to stay behind her ears. He'd miss the way she laughed at his jokes, even the bad ones—maybe especially the bad ones—because she knew that he knew just how bad they were. He'd miss the way she played basketball with the guys, giving it her all, knowing that she wasn't the best but never flagging in her enthusiasm. And he'd miss the long talks about absolutely nothing and absolutely everything—sweaty and tired, sprawled on the empty court, not wanting to take a shower because it would mean having to call an end to an evening.

"Mildred's right," he said aloud, swerving to avoid a teenaged driver who was in even more of a hurry than he was. "I'm in love."

Sam Wainwright in love. It was frightening, and he wasn't a man who spooked easy. There as a moment of terror as sure and as certain as when he was a child at the mercy of his dead mother's relatives who saw him as simply another mouth to feed, another burden to be endured.

And then after the moment of fear came a calm.

All that he would do, from this moment forward, would be for the love he felt for Patricia. He had found his purpose. And it wasn't to increase the profitability of Barrington Corporation or to hire the best people for the company. It wasn't to make Rex think he was good enough to have taken a chance on and it wasn't to prove to the mother he'd loved that he was a better man than his father had been.

Oh, no, his purpose was to love Patricia Peel. To be her man and to move her gray suits into his closet and tuck her hair behind her ears when it broke free. It was to make love to her and show her the tenderness and sweetness true loving could be. The thought of any other man having these liberties with his wife—his wife!—drove him to put his right foot on the floor and his car at an extra ten miles an hour.

As he spun around the corner at her street, he saw the taxi. Patricia's mom, balancing a large vase and a suitcase, stood on the curb. The driver, chewing a toothpick, walked down from the apartment building carrying a large copper temple bell.

Sam parked his car directly in front of the taxi.

"Hey!" the driver said in a bruising accent, roused to sufficient anger to take the toothpick out of his mouth. "I'm pullin' out soon as the little lady upstairs comes down."

Sam looked at Mrs. Peel.

"She's already got a sublet and an interview lined up with the Ritz-Carlton in Paris," she said matter-of-factly. "She is quite organized."

"She always is."

"But if you want to talk to her, I suppose I don't object. Our plane leaves in two hours, and even though I get waved through because I'm a diplomat, we still need... Hey! Let go of that!"

Sam snatched the suitcase from her hand and was

already halfway up the steps, and the Mexican-style gate slammed shut behind him.

"Tricia!" he shouted as he walked through the open door of her apartment and kicked it shut.

Crouched on the floor taping a moving box, she startled.

"Sam, don't say a word," she said, rising to her feet. "It's okay. I'm going home."

"You've never lived in Paris."

"I know, but home is where your family is."

"I'm your family. I'm your husband."

"That was just playacting."

"No, it wasn't. Whenever you say the words, those words, they come true. I love you," he said, striding toward her.

She backed away, keeping the cardboard box between them.

"Sam, you're just feeling sorry for me."

"I don't feel sorry for any of us, unless you get on that plane. I love you, Patricia. I just didn't know it before."

"Sam, I don't believe you," Patricia said. "I don't think you're lying to me, I just don't think you know what your feelings are. You're a gentleman who's trying to do the right thing, saving me from the humiliation of having the biggest darned crush in all of Arizona. Well, I don't need that protection. I have my feelings and I'm leaving with them, Sam. And you can tell the company whatever story you want. I didn't tell Mildred anything when I resigned."

"I don't want to tell anybody anything! I want my wife!"

"I was never your wife. We never consummated our marriage."

Sam sighed heavily, running a hand through his hair.

"When I left Barrington this morning, I wrote out a resignation letter and gave it to Mildred in an envelope that she's going to give Rex if I don't call her and tell her that we're both staying," Sam said.

"You don't have to do that. I resigned."

"If you won't let me be your husband, I'm going to leave Phoenix. It'll be your town. You don't have to go anywhere. I'll explain everything to Rex, about how it was my idea…"

"It wasn't your idea."

"It was, too. I'm the jerk."

"You're not a jerk. Everything you do you do because you're an honorable man. An honorable, wonderful man who tries so hard. And I'm leaving because I've loved you—too much."

"Patricia, you won't stay?"

"No."

"You don't have to run to Paris. Both of us know how important it is to have a home, a real home, a permanent home. You're happy at Barrington, happy with Phoenix. You stay. I'll go."

She softened.

"But your job is the most important thing to you."

He shook his head.

"It's you," he said. "If I walk out of Phoenix, but I know you're happy and that the damage I've done to you is diminished somehow, that'll have to do."

"You can't give up your job," Patricia said.

"Can and will. Because I love you."

She swiped tears from her cheeks.

"You can't love me," she wailed.

"Why not? What's so impossible about it?"

"I'm not pretty, I'm not stylish, I'm not sophisticated, I'm not..."

He had heard enough. He kicked aside the moving box and took her in his arms, steadying her shoulders as they convulsed with the force of her sobs.

"This is what I love," he said, tousling her hair. "This is what I've always loved. Even if I didn't have sense enough to know it."

She looked up at him, eyes glittering like emeralds. He kissed a tear that glistened on her lower lip. And then he kissed again, this time for real. This time swelling with the feelings he had too long denied.

"Patricia," he said hoarsely. "Put your arms around me. It's okay, baby, we're married. Remember?"

She linked her fingers around the belt loops on the back of his jeans. Her smile was wide and Sam knew he could die happy with that smile as his last image. She blushed, making her freckles pop! with sun-touched color.

"You're...you're...you're excited," she said.

"Of course I am."

She unbuttoned the top button of his shirt.

"Do you think twenty-nine is too old to be a virgin?" she asked mischievously.

"Honey, I think twenty-nine is just right."

Two hours later, Patricia bolted upright in bed.

"Sam, we have a problem," she said.

He stretched lazily and Patricia resisted the urge to splay her fingers on his firm, hard chest.

It would only get him going again, and while the prospect was delicious, it wouldn't help matters any.

"If we have a problem, I'm too happy to care," Sam said.

"No, darling, we have a real problem. Neither one of us has a job. I turned in my resignation. You told Mildred that you were resigning if you didn't call back."

He blinked twice.

"That's a problem," he agreed. "Because I was planning on buying you a new engagement ring."

In four minutes flat, they walked out onto the front lawn. Okay, Sam's shirt wasn't buttoned. And he had never located his socks, but his shoes were on his feet, his jeans were zipped and that had to count for something.

Patricia's mother stood leaning against the cab chewing a toothpick.

"I forgot all about you!" Patricia exclaimed. "I'm so sorry, Mom."

"Forget it. It's the first unreliable thing you've

done in your life. Shoulda started that when you were thirteen. Besides, I was having a good time,'' Mrs. Peel said, taking a toothpick out of her mouth. ''Did you know Igor here lived in Moscow when your father and I were posted there?''

''She good woman,'' Igor said, sticking his head out of the driver's-side window. ''Good diplomat.''

''We've been catching up on old times,'' Mrs. Peel said. ''And you look like you're not coming to Paris.''

''We need to find out if we still have jobs here,'' Sam said.

''Igor and I will put this stuff back in the apartment,'' Mrs. Peel said, sighing. ''And then I'm going to try to make my flight. Igor can drive fast. Be a good son-in-law or I'll use my diplomatic connections to have you deported...to Texas.''

''I promise to be good,'' Sam said.

After a flurry of hugs and kisses, Sam drove his new bride to the Barrington headquarters.

''Congratulations,'' the receptionist greeted them. ''I hear it was a beautiful wedding.''

''Thank you,'' Patricia said, breaking into a run to catch up with Sam.

They took the elevator up to the top floor. Sam only faltered once, at the door to Rex's office.

''If we don't keep our jobs, we'll manage,'' he said. ''Don't look so down. Being unemployed would just mean that we'd have more time for making love.''

He kissed her for luck and Patricia resisted the urge to hold on tight.

"Good morning," Rex said, looking up from his paperwork as they entered his office. "Don't you two lovebirds look happy!"

"Rex, did you get any...paperwork from us this morning?"

"Yes."

"Resignations?"

"Yes."

"Are you...accepting them?" Patricia asked.

"I'm totally baffled by them. I thought you two were happy here."

"We were. We are. But we've got a confession to make," Sam said.

"Oh, really? Will it take long?"

"Probably."

"Have a seat," Rex said, and he pressed a button on his speaker phone. "Mildred, hold my calls. Sam and Patricia have come to talk to me. Now, children," he said, directing his attention back to them, "what can I do for you?"

Sam held Patricia's hand, soothing her trembling with a tight squeeze.

"Rex, we lied to you," Sam said, certain that getting it out up front would be the most honorable thing to do. "We lied to you about being engaged."

"You weren't engaged?"

"No."

"Well, you're married now, so I suppose it

doesn't matter," Rex said, brightening. "Does this mean you have come back to work?"

"You don't understand. I lied to you. When you came to my office and told me you wanted to meet the woman I was going to marry, I wasn't engaged."

Rex drew his eyebrows together.

"You weren't?"

"No, I had been engaged to a woman named Melissa Stanhope."

"Of the silver mine Stanhopes?"

"Yes."

"Thank goodness you came to your senses. I would have fired you just for staying with her. She's a spoiled little number."

"But Rex, I asked Patricia to pretend to be my fiancée for your party just so that you would think I was engaged."

"We did it just to make sure that Sam's job was secure," Patricia added. "You had said that you would like the vice president in charge of personnel to have a rock-solid personal life."

The door to the office opened.

"I brought their letters of resignation," Mildred Van Hess said, approaching the desk. She held up a spaghettilike tangle of paper fresh from the shredder and dropped the pile in front of Rex.

"Oh, Mildred, I'm glad you took care of that," Rex said. "Are you two kids taking that honeymoon or not?"

"But Rex, I lied to you!" Sam protested. "It was wrong of me."

"Sam, are you married now?"

"Yes."

"Then what do I care about how it all came about?"

"Because you wanted the vice president of personnel to be married, and so I did this just to make sure that I'd stay in my job."

"I never wanted my vice president to be married," Rex said.

"You didn't?" Sam asked.

"You didn't?" Patricia asked.

"I just wanted to see my friend Sam happy before I left."

Sam blinked.

"Sam, you have a real good friend here," Patricia said. "A real good friend."

Sam looked at Patricia and then at Rex.

"If my words helped you find the love of your life, then I won't apologize for giving you the idea that I'd only want you to continue in your capacity of vice president if you were married," Rex said. "Patricia, remember, I told you I think that when you love someone, you should let them know. My mistake was that I didn't know you two hadn't let each other know."

"Does that mean we still have our jobs?" Patricia asked.

"Of course, you silly," Mildred said.

Sam squeezed Patricia's hand.

"I guess I needed to have some help at seeing you," he said, "even when you were right in front of me all along."

As he kissed her, Rex put his chin in his hand and sighed.

"My fondest retirement wish comes true. Sam is happy at last," he said, and then looked up at Mildred. "Ain't love grand?"

Mildred did a double take.

"Yes, Rex, it sure is."

Patricia shared a quiet, special glance with Sam. He looked at her, really looked at her—the way she'd always hoped, loving her and seeing all the love she had for him.

Women did it all the time. Asking out the man of their dreams. Taking chances. Falling in love. But Patricia had done it only once. Once in a lifetime.

With Sam, that's all she needed.

*   *   *   *   *

Don't miss Sophia's story,
I MARRIED THE BOSS!,
by Laura Anthony,
next month's
LOVING THE BOSS title,
available only in
Silhouette Romance.

SOMETIMES THE SMALLEST PACKAGES CAN LEAD TO THE BIGGEST SURPRISES!

February 1999
A VOW, A RING, A BABY SWING
by Teresa Southwick (SR #1349)

Pregnant and alone, Rosie Marchetti had just been stood up at the altar.
So family friend Steve Schafer stepped up the aisle and married her.
Now Rosie is trying to convince him that this family was meant to be....

May 1999
THE BABY ARRANGEMENT
by Moyra Tarling (SR #1368)

Jared McAndrew has been searching for his son, and when he discovers
Faith Nelson with his child he demands she come home with him. Can
Faith convince Jared that he has the wrong mother—but the right bride?

Enjoy these stories of love and family. And look for future
BUNDLES OF JOY titles from Leanna Wilson and Suzanne McMinn
coming in the fall of 1999.

BUNDLES OF JOY
only from

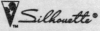

Available wherever Silhouette books are sold.

If you enjoyed what you just read,
then we've got an offer you can't resist!

Take 2 bestselling love stories FREE!

Plus get a FREE surprise gift!

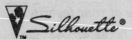

Coming in May 1999

BABY *Fever*

by
New York Times Bestselling Author

KASEY MICHAELS

When three sisters hear their biological
clocks ticking, they know it's
time for action.

But who will they get to father their babies?

Find out how the road to motherhood
leads to love in this brand-new collection.

Available at your favorite retail outlet.

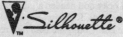

Silhouette
ROMANCE™

COMING NEXT MONTH

#1372 I MARRIED THE BOSS!—Laura Anthony
Loving the Boss

Sophia Shepherd wanted to marry the ideal man, and her new boss, Rex Michael Barrington III, was as dreamy as they came! But when an overheard conversation had him testing her feelings, Sophia had to prove she wanted more than just a dream....

#1373 HIS TEN-YEAR-OLD SECRET—Donna Clayton
Fabulous Fathers

Ten years of longing were over. Tess Galloway had returned to claim the child she'd thought lost to her forever. But Dylan Minster, her daughter's father and the only man she'd ever loved, would not let Tess have her way without a fight, and without her heart!

#1374 THE RANCHER AND THE HEIRESS—Susan Meier
Texas Family Ties

City girl Alexis MacFarland wasn't thrilled about spending a year on a ranch—even if it meant she'd inherit half of it! But one look at ranch owner Caleb Wright proved it wouldn't be *that* bad, *if* she could convince him she'd be his cowgirl for good.

#1375 THE MARRIAGE STAMPEDE—Julianna Morris
Wranglers & Lace

Wrangler Merrie Foster and stockbroker Logan Kincaid were *nothing* alike. She wanted kids and country life, and he wanted wealth and the city. But when they ended up in a mock engagement, would the sparks between them overcome their differences?

#1376 A BRIDE IN WAITING—Sally Carleen
On the Way to a Wedding

Stand in for a missing bride? Sara Martin didn't mind, especially as a favor for Dr. Lucas Daniels. But when her life became filled with wedding plans and stolen kisses, Sara knew she wanted to change from stand-in bride to wife forever!

#1377 HUSBAND FOUND—Martha Shields
Family Matters

Single mother Emma Lockwood needed a job...and R. D. Johnson was offering one. Trouble was, Rafe was Emma's long-lost husband—and he didn't recognize her! Could she help him recover his memory—and the love they once shared?